Axis
Church
vs.
Eris
Church

KONOSUBA:
GOD'S BLESSING ON THIS
WONDERFUL WORLD!
8

Aqua

"This year, we're going to cancel the Eris Festival and have an Aqua Festival instead!"

"What's with that hottie in the middle?! I've never seen anyone like her! She's not just devilishly attractive—she's a straight-up devil girl!"

"Yes, yes, a thousand times yes! Pretty face, great body, and a noble?!"

Succubus?

Aigis

Wiz

"Man, I wanna get with a high-level lady like that! She looks so cozy and huggable!"

"...it won't even need me anymore."

"I hope
one day
the world
will be so
peaceful..."

KONOSUBA: GOD'S BLESSING ON THIS WONDERFUL WORLD! 8

Axis Church vs. Eris Church

CONTENTS

Illustrations/Kurone Mishima
Design/Yuko Yaoya +
Nanafushi Nakamura
(Mushikago Graphics)

KONOSUBA: GOD'S BLESSING ON THIS WONDERFUL WORLD!

Axis Church vs. Eris Church

8

NATSUME AKATSUKI

ILLUSTRATION BY
KURONE MISHIMA

YEN ON
NEW YORK

KONOSUBA: GOD'S BLESSING ON THIS WONDERFUL WORLD! 8

NATSUME AKATSUKI

Translation by Kevin Steinbach
Cover art by Kurone Mishima

KONO SUBARASHII SEKAI NI SHUKUFUKU WO!, Volume 8: AKUSIZU KYODAN VS ERISU KYODAN
Copyright © 2016 Natsume Akatsuki, Kurone Mishima
First published in Japan in 2016 by KADOKAWA CORPORATION, Tokyo.
English translation rights arranged with KADOKAWA CORPORATION, Tokyo, through TUTTLE-MORI AGENCY, INC., Tokyo.

English translation © 2019 by Yen Press, LLC

Yen On
1290 Avenue of the Americas
New York, NY 10104

Visit us at yenpress.com
facebook.com/yenpress
twitter.com/yenpress
yenpress.tumblr.com
instagram.com/yenpress

First Yen On Edition: April 2019

Yen On is an imprint of Yen Press, LLC.
The Yen On name and logo are trademarks of Yen Press, LLC.

The publisher is not responsible for websites (or their content) that are not owned by the publisher.

Library of Congress Cataloging-in-Publication Data
Names: Akatsuki, Natsume, author. | Mishima, Kurone, 1991– illustrator. | Steinbach, Kevin, translator.
Title: Konosuba, God's blessing on this wonderful world! / Natsume Akatsuki ; illustration by Kurone Mishima ; translation by Kevin Steinbach.
Other titles: Kono subarashi sekai ni shukufuku wo. English
Description: First Yen On edition. | New York, NY : Yen On, 2017–
Identifiers: LCCN 2016052009 | ISBN 9780316553377 (v. 1 : paperback) |
ISBN 9780316468701 (v. 2 : paperback) | ISBN 9780316468732 (v. 3 : paperback) |
ISBN 9780316468763 (v. 4 : paperback) | ISBN 9780316468787 (v. 5 : paperback) |
ISBN 9780316468800 (v. 6 : paperback) | ISBN 9780316468824 (v. 7 : paperback) |
ISBN 9780316468855 (v. 8 : paperback)
Subjects: CYAC: Fantasy. | Future life—Fiction. | Adventure and adventurers—Fiction. |
BISAC: FICTION / Fantasy / General.
Classification: LCC PZ7.1.A38 Ko 2017 | DDC [Fic]—dc23
LC record available at https://lccn.loc.gov/2016052009

ISBNs: 978-0-316-46885-5 (paperback)
978-0-316-46886-2 (ebook)

10 9 8 7 6 5 4 3 2 1

LSC-C

Printed in the United States of America

KONOSUBA: GOD'S BLESSING ON THIS WONDERFUL WORLD!

Axis Church vs. Eris Church

Characters

Darkness

Age 18
Job Crusader

A female knight who specializes in defense and enjoys being beaten up by monsters. Daughter of the Dustiness family, a powerful noble house. Special skill: fantasizing.

Aqua

Age Unknown
Job Arch-priest

A goddess who gives guidance to the young and deceased. Goes to a parallel world with Kazuma to defeat the Demon King. Likes wine. Special skill: party tricks.

Megumin

Age 14
Job Arch-wizard

Exceptionally talented, even by Crimson Magic Clan standards. Obsessed with the überpowerful spell Explosion, she is neither capable of nor interested in using any other magic. Favorite thing: Explosion. Special skill: Explosion. Hobby: Explosion.

Wiz

Age 20
Job Shopkeeper

Vanir

Age Unknown
Job Terrible Demon, Shopkeeper

Kazuma Satou

Age 16
Job Adventurer

An adventurer and *hikikomori* (in any world) who brought Aqua to their current plane. Has already given up on defeating the Demon King.

Chris

Age 15?
Job Thief

Eris

Age Unknown
Job Goddess

Prologue

I wasn't big on the culture festivals in school, so I never dreamed I'd find myself helping with a celebration in an alternate world.

Even the Axis disciples, normally people to be feared, were as sweet as pet kittens. They had a lot riding on this festival.

I couldn't help a breath of admiration for what I saw before me. In the light of the scattered bonfires, this other-world celebration looked truly fantastical.

Right in the middle of it all was something that would have looked perfectly normal in Japan but seemed out of place in this world: classic Japanese vendors' stalls.

The people of this world had dreamed up every kind of shop, and it was obvious they were all genuinely enjoying themselves. It didn't matter that the festival lasted only a few days out of the whole year.

There were demi-humans and elves and dwarves.

Undead and demons and goddesses, too.

"Kazuma, Kazuma! I'm so glad we were able to have this festival."

* * *

Aqua, happily watching the goings-on, took a second to glance back at me.

"Thank you for helping the Axis Church."

Her innocent smile shone against the incredible backdrop of the festival, and her words, for once, came straight from the heart.

Chapter 1

May There Be Honor for This Dragon!

1

I was pretty flummoxed by what was going on—despite the fact that I'd brought it on myself.

I was in a cozy little café on the outskirts of Axel Town.

And now...

Now, she was sitting all but frozen in front of me, a smile on her face: Chris... Or rather...

"What in the world are you doing here, Lady Eris?"

...the goddess Eris, whose identity I had finally guessed.

The day after I had rescued Darkness from being wed in order to pay off a debt, Axel's governor, Alderp, had mysteriously disappeared. Almost as if on cue, a slew of evidence had been discovered proving the man's evil deeds and general bad behavior.

The next governor of Axel was to be Darkness's father.

Along with that, Darkness's debts that I had taken on, and all the other money I had paid—such as the cost of repairs to the town after defeating the Demon King's general Beldia or the cost of repairs to the governor's mansion after defeating Mobile Fortress Destroyer—all of that was apparently going to come back to me.

Alderp's son, Balter, to whom Darkness had *also* nearly gotten married, had been cleared of any association with his father's wrong-doing and hadn't been punished; he was going to be Darkness's dad's assistant.

Because her father wasn't yet fully recovered from his illness, Darkness was appointed as the acting governor, but at the moment, she had shut herself up in her house and still hadn't come out. Maybe that selfish brat didn't like the new nickname I'd given her.

Anyway, I was bringing Chris up to speed on all this…

"I'm not Lady Eris; I'm Lady Chris."

I had started to suspect that Chris and Eris were the same person and tried to trick Chris into admitting as much, but she just kept smiling and repeating the same nonsensical phrase. So I said to Chris—I mean, Eris…

"Hey, there's something I've been wondering about. When you're in this body, Lady Eris, you always refer to your senior, Aqua, so politely. But you just call Darkness and Megumin by their names."

"……I'm a very pious and upright thief, the kind who would donate to the church some of the money I took. I couldn't refer to an Arch-priest like Miss Aqua without being polite."

Eris looked away from me, and she scratched at the scar on her cheek as if she thought it would throw me off the trail—but her excuse really was a stretch.

"You know, Lady Eris has the same habit of scratching her cheek when she's not sure what to do."

At that, my friend's finger suddenly fell still.

"Let me ask again: What *are* you doing here?" I said to the suddenly silent Eris.

"…Heh-heh, that's Mr. Kazuma Satou for you. In fact, that's exactly why you're fit to be my lowly assistant." Eris stood abruptly and started talking in a theatrical tone, like a criminal who'd been found out by a famous detective. "Indeed, it is as you suspect. Sometimes I'm an adventurer. Other times, a noble thief. And still other times, one of Darkness's friends. But my true identity is…!"

"Wow, you're really getting into this, Lady Eris."

"…Or maybe you're just surprisingly calm, my dear Kazuma… I guess I've been found out— Oh well! Nothing to do but tell you the whole story…"

Eris sat back down, and suddenly her expression was much more serious than before. It wasn't the face of the devil-may-care thief I knew—I was looking at the most venerated goddess in this entire world.

But as for me, I said:

"Gosh, I can't believe you're actually Lady Eris, Chief! You two have such different personalities and even different manners of speaking. Oh, um, please allow me to apologize for stealing your underwear the first time we met, Lady Eris."

"…"

The somber atmosphere was completely lost on me; instead, I apologized for what I had done during our first meeting.

Eris looked like she wanted to speak, but in the end, her mouth just twitched, and she said nothing at all.

"Now that the cat's outta the bag, I guess there were other telltale signs. Like that time when we were going to go into Khiel's Dungeon, and I tried to get you to teach me some Thief skills, and you said, 'A senior I owe a lot to made a crazy request of me, and I'm pretty busy right now.'"

Looking back, I can see why she was so busy.

"It got nuts for you because of the way Aqua demanded you bring me back to life after I was killed by General Winter, right? …Oh, something else I have to apologize for. When you broke in that one time, Lady Eris, and I captured you, I did cop a couple of feels. Sorry about that."

"All right! That's history now! You don't have to bring up every little thing!" Eris pounded the table, blushing faintly. Then she gave a small sigh, glanced around furtively, and whispered, "And please stop calling me Lady Eris when I'm in this body, Kazuma—I mean, Lowly Assistant. And just talk to me casually, like you've been doing. Don't be so deferential. Just treat me as Chris."

"...If you say so, Chris. Fine. So you gonna answer my question anytime soon? Why did you come down here? Why does a goddess masquerade as a thief? For that matter, which is the real you?"

"Okay, hang on—one question at a time!" Chris glanced around again, coughed discreetly, and frowned. "All right, from the top... I guess one of the reasons I'm here is so I can look for the Sacred Treasures."

The Sacred Treasures.

Extremely powerful cheat items given to people who had been sent to this world. It seemed one of Lady Eris's major reasons for being around here was to find items that had lost their owners and collect them so they could be given to new people who were sent here.

"I see; so being a thief is the best way to get those items back. But unlike a certain goddess I know who spends every day eating and sleeping, you really work hard at your job... You said that was 'one of the reasons' you're here. You have others?"

At that, Chris's serious expression lightened for a moment. "Well, and becoming friends with a young noblewoman who prayed for companionship..." She gave a shy little smile and scratched her cheek gently.

Darkness's dad had mentioned this. He said that after she became an adventurer, Darkness went to the Church of Eris every day to pray that she would find some friends to adventure with. And then, one day, she met Chris on her way home from church.

"...Wow. You're a real goddess, aren't you, Lady Eris?"

"I said, stop calling me that! ...E-er, anyway, I enjoyed adventuring with Darkness, too. This thing about my true identity, it's just between us, okay? Please make sure no one finds out, especially Darkness."

She scratched her cheek again, looking away. For some reason, everything she did struck me as even cuter than usual—maybe because

I knew now that I was sitting across from Eris. Was this what they called wearing goddess-colored glasses?

From guiding dead people to finding Sacred Treasures to befriending her own followers, she was one hard worker. I thought of a certain goddess—one who was eating snacks immediately after *I* died—who could stand to learn a thing or two from her.

"As for your last question, about which personality is really mine…" Chris gave a teasing little smile. "Which do you like better? Chris or Eris?"

"I love them both."

"Huh? …E-er, d-do you, now? I didn't expect you to sound so certain. I took you for the type to hesitate and stutter just a little more when he confessed his love for a girl." She couldn't look at me again; instead, she reflexively opened and closed the salt container on the table.

"I wasn't exactly confessing my love, just talking about personal preferences… There's you, Chief, with your tomboyish appeal, and the sweet, comforting Lady Eris. It's pretty hard to choose between the two… Hey! Maybe if you switched between Chris and Eris each day, I could get to know both sides of you! Kind of like double-dipping! Incredible: Lady Eris, a one-woman harem! Please go out with me…"

"You're the worst! You're worse than the worst! And I told you to stop with the Lady Eris stuff!"

I caught the saltshaker Chris flung at me, feeling at ease with this banter. For some reason, knowing I was talking to Eris made it easy to say things like *love* and *please go out with me.*

Was it because she was Eris—a goddess, someone who was out of reach almost by definition? Or was it because she was Chris, someone I had joined in doing stupid stuff like forming a thief gang? I didn't know which it was, but this mysterious connection felt really…nice.

"*Sigh…* For goodness' sake. I thought I was going to enjoy finally revealing the long-hidden secret of my identity. Talk about a waste…"

"I've only got one kind of feeling right now, and that's a bad one.

Don't tell me you're here to beg me to go Sacred Treasure hunting with you again."

Chris responded to my wary remark with a big grin. "That's my lowly assistant, quick on the uptake! So the Sacred Treasure I'm looking for this time is a set of holy armor called Aigis. It actually goes with the holy shield Aegis, but so far I've only been able to locate the armor…"

"Nope! I don't wanna hear it! I've had enough dangers, scrapes, and crises! Look, I've been picking up some pretty positive vibes from Megumin recently, and even Darkness seems to be interested in me for once! I've got so much money I don't even need to work! All I wanna do is lead a life of decadence and flirt with my party members!"

"Listen to you! Weren't you asking *me* to go out with you just a minute ago?! Come on—you're the only one I can ask about this! H-hey, don't plug your ears; your chief is giving you an order!"

Chris shook me—I had indeed plugged my ears and lain down across the table—and wailed. The handful of customers and staff looked over at the commotion. Chris must have noticed it, too, because she finally quieted down.

Just when I thought she would let it go, she looked slowly up at me…

"Mr. Kazuma Satou, I beg of you… Won't you help me, for the sake of this world…?"

Sitting across from me in a pose of supplication was the goddess Eris… Or rather, Chris, wearing Eris's disappointed face.

…*Lady Eris, that's not fair.*

2

And that's how I ended up in a team with Chris again.

A few days later, in the living room of my mansion…

"Dear friends. Humans are a species capable of holding conversation. So let us talk about this."

*   *   *

Vanir was sitting in the middle of the room, held in place by a powerful binding spell. Aqua and Wiz were sitting hardly an inch away on either side of him, so close that they were practically touching him, both frowning heavily and staring him in the face.

In front of him was Darkness—the girl who had so long holed up in her own mansion but had recently decided to start coming out again—also frowning, arms folded across her chest as she stood imposingly above him.

Darkness had been saved from having to marry Alderp, and I had gotten all my money back. Personally, I thought it was a matter of all's well that ends well, but...

"You're the one who benefited most from all this fuss. Lucky you, getting the chance to buy Kazuma's merchandise nice and cheap... Word gets around, you know? I heard how you were able to resell the intellectual property you got from Kazuma at a huge profit. I'll bet you knew a less ridiculously complicated way to solve these problems. How about the truth now, huh?" Throughout her entire diatribe, Aqua held protectively to the egg she had named Emperor Zel.

"Mr. Vanir, how could you have kept all this information a secret from me? You bought up every single one of Mr. Kazuma's ideas cheaply, then sold them again? Unbelievable...! Oh, what am I going to do? I never imagined all that money in our safe came at Mr. Kazuma's expense...! I'd love to return it, but it's already—!" Wiz covered her face, apologizing mournfully.

Vanir seemed to take a certain pity at the sight of his employer apologizing so profusely.

"Now, now, calm down, O yakuza lady and deadbeat shopkeep. Was there another way to solve that problem? Well, technically, yes...there... was...but...? ...Wait. What did you say, you deadbeat shopkeep?" Vanir stopped trying to placate Aqua and Wiz. "What happened to the money I put in that safe? That was not an amount that could be used in the blink of an eye."

Wiz looked up from her hands, and suddenly, her face was shining. "Oh, that! You should be proud, Mr. Vanir. Guess what? While I was looking after the store, a valued regular brought in a big load of manatite crystals. They were willing to sell them at half the market value, so I bought as many as I could with the money in the safe! This time I really did buy something good! From what I saw, those things have so much magical power that they have to be the purest manatite!"

Manatite is a substance that can restore an amount of magic in proportion to the quality of the crystal. It's awfully expensive for a consumable item, so naturally, there was zero demand for it in a town full of beginning adventurers like this one.

I could only feel bad for Vanir as he sat there absorbing Wiz's story.

I decided I'd try asking him a question of my own.

"So, uh, not that I think you necessarily planned all of this. But Aqua said Darkness's old man was cursed by a demon... And you're the only demon around here, right?"

Yes, this was the reason we had suspected Vanir to begin with...

"Bwa-ha-ha! Behold, I say, far be it from me to place a curse that might endanger someone's life! The bestower of that curse was another demon, one famous for being not quite right in the head. He says and does all sorts of strange things."

"That pretty much sounds like you," I said.

Aqua and Wiz grabbed Vanir's shoulders from either side, while Darkness, the daughter of the man cursed in this recent incident, stood implacably before him.

"Hold, knaves! Do you mean to imply that one of my revered station would say or do anything that would cause you to confuse me with a broken demon like that? Very well, let us discuss! I will admit that I, *ahem*, took the scenic route in resolving these events. And I further acknowledge that I orchestrated these developments in order to feast upon the animosity produced when that lord saw his bride stolen away before his very eyes. But I implore you to listen—in particular, the girl standing squarely before me, who, thanks to recent events, was made blindingly aware of her feelings for this young man and whose at-home dress has consequently become skimpier than ever bef—"

"Waaaaaaahhhhh! I take revenge for my fatherrrr!"

"H-hey, my mask! Don't you try to destroy my mask! And your father isn't even dead!"

Darkness had launched herself at Vanir, who was still restrained by Wiz and Aqua, and very nearly succeeded in smashing his mask to pieces.

As I sat there with my proverbial popcorn, I felt Megumin tug on my clothing.

"Kazuma, it seems we've now confirmed that Vanir was behind all this, and I'd like to go out and do my explosion for the day. Would you be so kind as to come with me?"

"Yeah, sure. It doesn't look like this is going to wrap up anytime soon. Maybe they'll have cooled off by the time we get home."

I grabbed the minimal equipment I would need and headed off with Megumin.

3

"I haven't thanked you yet, have I, Kazuma?"

Megumin spoke up from beside me as we walked. We were a little ways out of town, following a path toward a mountain valley that boasted lots of exposed rock.

"Thank me? Thank me for what? …Ah, you mean when I went and apologized to the parents after you made their kid cry? That's water under the bridge. But next time, don't bully a little kid just because they made fun of your name, okay?"

"Such a ridiculous thing is not what I'm referring to! And furthermore, I have no fault in that incident. That child was wrong to mock the name of a member of the Crimson Magic Clan!"

While Megumin was still fuming, we reached our "explosion spot."

We came here virtually every day; it was sort of Megumin's equivalent of a hole-in-the-wall. Don't ask what kind of hole, but there were big chunks of rock scattered everywhere. I got the impression this was less about getting off an explosion and more about satisfying her thirst for wanton destruction.

If we had run into any monsters on the way, I had been thinking I would have her blow them away to help gain experience points—but sadly, the path was clear.

"I wanted to thank you for helping Darkness, Kazuma."

Megumin had spotted an attractive boulder at the foot of the mountain and pattered over to inspect it; she didn't even spare me a glance as she talked. It looked like we had found today's target.

"Oh, that. Darkness owes me an awful lot—I couldn't just let her leave the party like that. And anyway, I'm used to cleaning up your messes by now. No need to thank me at this point." I shrugged, speaking casually.

Megumin backed away from the rock and chuckled. "Even so. As I believe I told you back at Crimson Magic Village…" She turned away from me, raising her staff in the direction of the boulder. "…Despite all your complaining, when push comes to shove, you are always there for us. I love that about you."

She said it so easily…

"…Hey, I really need you to stop throwing around that word and any others like it. We're not talking about the weather. I don't know how to react. If you say things like *love* way too easily, you're gonna cause a misunderstanding. Give it to me straight. Is this a serious confession?" I spoke as calmly as I could, trying not to betray the trembling in my heart.

"I wonder," Megumin said, her back still to me, and giggled. "I'm sure you would *love* to know."

…No really, was she serious? Or was she teasing me again?

Hang on. Think, Kazuma Satou.

For a while now, Megumin had been giving off vibes that she had feelings for me. I didn't know why she would choose now of all times to fall in love, but if I had to guess, it might have something to do with my helping Darkness.

This might sound immodest, but even I have to admit I was pretty cool. Yeah, this was just like what would happen to the protagonist of a romance novel. I did spend the night after I rescued Darkness in bed with the covers pulled over my head, trembling at the thought that I might be executed for what I had done, but looking back on it now, I guess I actually had been pretty heroic.

…For that matter, I had been living in the same house with these girls for quite a while now. Not only was it not surprising that one of them would finally start to show some flowering of affection for me, it was downright shocking that the place hadn't turned into my personal harem yet.

Sing it! Sing it, Kazuma Satou! Victory is within your grasp! Be not afraid!

You shan't be refused or isolated! …You…shouldn't be, anyway…!

I—I wouldn't be, would I?

Right! Go! You'll be fine—just be courageous!

"Well…I'm happy you feel that way, Megumin. I mean, I don't exactly hate you, eith—"

"*EXPLOSION!!*"

4

"What's the matter with you? What are you pouting about?" Megumin asked like the oblivious protagonist of some novel as I carried her along on my back. She had been jabbering about it all the way home.

It's not like I felt anything for Megumin. What did I care if she totally killed the mood?

Sure, she was nice enough to look at, but she was also a weirdo who would never shut up about explosions. Other people might've gotten caught up in the moment—but nope, not me!

"Kazuma, were you saying something in the instant I cast my explosion magic? I couldn't hear you over the blast, but it seemed like you were trying to say something important."

"Oh, it was nothing! Believe me—I don't feel anything for you!"

"Why the *tsundere* act? You're sending some very mixed signals. Pull yourself together. When we get back to the mansion, I'll give you an extra helping of that pudding I bought."

"...Two extra helpings," I said as I turned the doorknob of our house.

Then I opened the door.

"I can't do that. With Aqua and Darkness, there's only one extra serving, so someone wouldn't be able to have any—"

Megumin stopped midsentence.

...And I was silent, too.

We entered the house to find...

"Give him baaack! Please! Give back my sweet little Emperor Zel!! Waaaaah, give him back!"

"Bwa-ha-ha-ha-ha-ha-ha-ha! Serves you right, O goddess betrayed; your precious pet is— Bwa-ha— Ahh, dammit! St-stop that! Don't you follow me, you awful bird; go back to your owner!"

We discovered Aqua, weeping and pounding on Vanir's back.

...And there on the carpet lay Wiz and Darkness, both out cold. Wiz, in fact, was starting to disappear a little.

Then there was what was almost certainly the source of Aqua's bawling.

Down by the feet of the relentlessly pounded Vanir...

"Peep!"

...was what was unmistakably a chick.

It was trying to cuddle up to Vanir's feet.

"Okay. Somebody tell me what's going on here," I said, letting Megumin down on the couch. I made Aqua and Vanir sit down so they could explain the situation to me. I didn't know why Wiz was fading away and Darkness was lying on the floor unconscious, but I assumed it had something to do with these two.

There was no way one of Aqua's attacks could put Darkness out of commission, and nothing Vanir did would cause Wiz to disappear.

Aqua and Vanir sat down on the floor, and immediately, each pointed a finger at the other.

""S/he did it!"" they chorused, then glared at each other from close range.

Aqua furrowed her brows and ground her teeth, making her anger obvious. Vanir's actual expression was a mystery from behind his mask, but his mouth was pulled into a tight line.

And a tiny yellow ball was perching on Vanir's knee.

…*It's total chaos in here. What am I going to do?*

The only option was to hear both sides of the story.

"Listen! Listen to me, Kazuma! While we were interrogating Ugly Mask here, he suddenly went berserk and attacked us! He was all, 'Vanir Something-or-Other!' I smacked him back with magic, but then it hit Darkness, too, and knocked her out, so I used purification magic! And *he* used Wiz as a shield, and that's why she's disappearing! And just when I was thinking my only choice was to wipe this guy out of existence…!"

I see.

I don't get it at all.

"Bwa-ha-ha-ha-ha, underhanded woman who presents only the evidence most convenient to her! Along with that muscle-headed girl and my traitorous shopkeeper, she assumed that my predominantly innocent self was guilty! Without so much as a lawyer to defend me, this trial was null, void, and unacceptable, and so I used my Vanir Death Ray attack in self-defense. It was this woman who deflected it and caused it to hit her buff friend, whereupon she further decided, altogether outrageously, to attack me with magic, so I grabbed my shopkeeper as a barrier and managed to escape unscathed. And just when I was thinking my only choice was to put an end to this battle that would echo through the ages…!"

""Emperor Zel hatched.""

Ah, I see.
I don't get it at all.

5

Zeltman Kingsford.

Apple of the eye of the goddess of water, chosen from among the vast panoply of eggs in the world, of lineage strong and true, and…a chick.

"A fine name. A strong name overflowing with intimidation. It's no surprise he should cleave to my person."

"Of course he has a good name, and what do you mean, cleave? I can't quite excuse the fact that he does seem to like you, but this little one was chosen by me—a deity! He's destined to be the emperor of the dragons."

As Aqua and Vanir exchanged barbs where they sat on the carpet, the chick sat absolutely motionless.

He looked exactly like chicks I had seen in Japan. He had all the vulnerability of a newborn, yet he didn't seem the least bit intimidated by the goddess and the demon arguing right above him; instead, he sat proudly on the great demon's knee, staring at him unwaveringly.

Zeltman Kingsford.

Nicknamed Emperor Zel, on the hope that he would indeed one day become the ruler of dragonkind.

I plucked Emperor Zel off Vanir's knee.

"So what's the plan? Fried chicken for dinner tonight?"

"No! Kazuma, this just goes to show what a monster you are! I swear, this masked demon is more human than you sometimes!"

"No need to be so rude, O pitiful cuckold. Do not equate myself, who keeps an eye on neighborhood safety while the children are coming home from school, with this man who, with the departure of our awful governor, now ranks as the most depraved inhabitant of Axel."

I think I'm gonna cry.

...Anyway, I'd more or less gotten ahold of the situation. Basically, Emperor Zel hatched while Aqua and Vanir were fighting, and he imprinted on Vanir.

I held Emperor Zel cupped in both hands, Megumin eyeing me jealously from the sofa. I guess she wanted to pet him. I passed the emperor to her and went to check on Wiz and Darkness.

"...I wonder why newborn animals are so adorable," Megumin said, holding Zel carefully in her hands. "Is it in hopes that predators will take pity on them and not eat them?"

Meanwhile, I was heading over to Wiz and Darkness.

...Wiz was looking a little translucent, but there was nothing I could do about that. Instead, I hoisted up Darkness and gave her a few gentle slaps on the cheek, but she didn't wake up.

"Anyway, you're a bad influence on Emperor Zel, so scurry on home," Aqua said to Vanir. "I'm trying to make sure Zel learns only the very best lessons... Look! Look at Megumin's relaxed expression as she gazes at Emperor Zel. Amazing. Just born, and Zel is already a lady-killer. They say heroes love the fairer sex, so I think this bodes well for his future!"

"Hmph! You don't have to encourage me to show myself out. Thanks to that deadweight—and now passed-out—shopkeeper, all the money I so diligently hoarded has turned into a bunch of rocks. Well, humans. If you come by some pocket change, I hope you'll patronize Wiz's Magical Item Shoppe!" He grabbed Wiz, now about half-vanished, and said, "Excuse me, but could I have some sugar water? At this rate, she'll be changing classes from a pseudo-Lich to an extinct one. Bring me some nutritional supplements—maybe if we douse her with sugar water or something, she'll revive, like a rhinoceros beetle."

I wondered what Wiz's day-to-day life must be like.

Vanir made for the kitchen as he spoke, but…

"Huh?! Wh-what's wrong, Emperor Zel?!" Megumin was startled when the chick began flapping around in her hands; she put him gently on the carpet.

What, even Megumin doesn't feel weird calling him Emperor Zel?

He's a chick.

So why does he get the most important-sounding name out of all of us?

"Hrm…?"

As we all watched, the yellow fluff ball with the imposing name toddled over to Vanir and cuddled up to his shoe.

Aqua grabbed hold of me. "Waaah! Emperor Zel's been stolen from me! Kazuma! Dear Kazumaaa! Please slay that masked demon and get me my Emperor Zel back!"

"Why me? You're in a better position to defeat him than I am. Plus, that's a chick. Not a dragon. Doesn't that bother you?"

At that, Aqua went over to where Zel was huddled up by Vanir and held him lovingly to her chest.

"If I were to destroy the masked demon he likes so much, Emperor Zel would hate me. And you may be too blind to see it, Kazuma, but this is an exceedingly rare type of dragon that's covered in fur, called a Shaggy Dragon. No doubt about it."

"I understand not wanting to admit that you got had, but give it up already. That thing is obviously and without question just a normal chick."

As Vanir was getting Wiz some sugar water, he watched Aqua plug her ears and pretend not to hear me.

"Hey," I said to them, "Darkness doesn't look like she's coming around. Is this normal?"

Vanir peered at Darkness, puzzled. "Hmm. Your goddess supposedly healed her wounds. But it's rather staggering that she took a blast from my Vanir Death Ray and is still breathing. It's called a death ray

for a reason. Normally, people die from it. It is *I* who would like to ask *you* how she is still alive. She must have monstrous Magic Defense... But this incident is to the discredit of myself, who swore not to harm any person. When she awakens, ask her for me just how muscle-headed she is."

"That's gonna get me slapped," I said. "Eh, never mind. The only question is what we do with this little guy." I looked down at the yellow fluff ball, who still refused to leave Vanir's feet.

I was starting to think it would be just as well to let Vanir take him home.

"Hmm. I cannot blame him for being so attached to me, idol of the local housewives, but there is an unbridgeable species gap between birds and demons. I apologize to Emperor Zel, but he must give up on me."

"Uh, I think he thinks you're his father."

This caused Vanir to grunt thoughtfully. "...No choice, then. Hey, where does Emperor Zel sleep?"

Aqua pointed to the couch without a word.

Hey, don't let the chick sleep there.

Vanir plucked Emperor Zel up off the floor and plopped down on the sofa. Zel sat still, which he seemed to do only in Vanir's hands.

Boy, he was really convinced Vanir was his dad.

Vanir leaned over as if giving the chick a hug, and then, with the bird clutched in his hands...

"Skin Shed!"

He intoned the words almost musically and suddenly split himself in two.

Emperor Zel remained in the hands of Vanir's double, so he couldn't see the real Vanir. Our ready-for-anything demon held up a hand, while his unmoving husk clasped the chick.

"I believe this is good-bye for today."

"I keep thinking I've gotten used to the creatures in this world, but you really take the cake."

6

It was the day after our new mascot had joined the household.

"...Hey, Kazuma. Could you stop eating fried eggs in front of Emperor Zel? I can't help thinking he looks a little scared of you." Aqua was feeding Zel bread crumbs.

"He's a dragon, isn't he? Then he doesn't have to be scared of me... More to the point, do something with Vanir's shell already. It's like having him sitting right there. I'm losing my appetite just looking at it."

I gestured with my chopsticks at Vanir's empty shell, which had taken on the role of Zel's bed, and next to which Aqua was now sitting. The body was empty, but it looked exactly like Vanir and retained a certain amount of his personal charisma; even just sitting there, it was totally creepy.

"What am I supposed to do? Emperor Zel likes it so much... More to the *real* point, I wonder what's up with *her* right now."

As Zel pecked at her fingers (which looked pretty painful), Aqua glanced over to the corner of the room.

"Looks to me like she's scared of our little yellow fluff ball."

Curled up and cowering in the corner was Chomusuke.

I had been worried that the black fluff ball might eat the yellow fluff ball, so this outcome was surprising, to say the least.

"It has to do with magical power," Megumin said, chewing on some toast and fixing Zel with a stare.

"Magical power?"

"Yes, magical power. I feel an incredible magical energy from Emperor Zel."

...From the fluff ball?

"During the egg's incubation, Aqua and I, along with Vanir and Wiz and all the top-class magic-users in town, poured our magical energy into it. It's well-known that dragon parents warm their eggs with magical energy so that the offspring are born with powerful magic themselves, and it's fascinating to see that the same thing happens with chickens. We should probably report this to the people raising dragons out on the dragon farm."

So what was her point? Was this critter really going to become the creature of legend Aqua claimed he was?

"So if we raise him right, he could become our ace in the hole against the Demon King and his—"

"No. No, he couldn't, because he is a chick," Megumin said. "He can't use magic, and therefore he can't magically fly like a dragon or use magical breath weapons like a dragon."

......

"You don't think one day he'll suddenly manifest some incredible power, or that he'll be extra tough, or—?"

"Oh, definitely not. Sometimes large amounts of magical energy can slow the aging process and extend one's life, but he is just a chick, after all. He won't awaken to any special powers. The best we can hope for is that maybe he'll scare off wild monsters with his large amount of magic."

What a waste.

"Oh! That's it! I can use Drain Touch on him; he'll be better than manatite."

"I'm afraid that won't work, either, because he is just a chick. If you accidentally Drain too much and cut into his vitality instead, you could kill him easily."

What to do; what to do?

"...I wonder if I would get a big magic boost if I ate him."

"...Perhaps. He's so cute that I don't really want to do it, but if there's a chance of boosting our magic, it might be worth a try."

"Don't look at my sweet baby like that! Get away! Darkness, protect Emperor Zel from these predators!"

Darkness had finished her breakfast and was peacefully sipping some tea; she only regarded us with a slight smile. "...Heh-heh.

Watching you guys, I finally feel like I'm truly home. Kazuma, Megumin, don't bully Aqua too much, please. We can all live in harmony together now. There's no need to fight. Just be friends." Her smile grew wider; she looked completely at peace.

"...You sure went from shut-in to cheery in no time," I said. "Already over the trauma of being dumped by that governor? A virgin divorcée is a new one to me, but hey, you just keep seeing how many weird distinctions you can pile up."

"He didn't dump me—he disappeared, and it's obviously because he ran away when his misdeeds were found out!" Darkness shot back. "And I'm not a divorcée. My family record is still clean." She grinned.

"...? ...Oh! She used her noble status to alter her family registry! Get a load of this hypocrisy, Megumin. She always used to crow about how the Dustiness family didn't take advantage of their position to do anything wrong, but when she's cornered, suddenly here we are!"

"Darkness has indeed changed substantially, hasn't she?" Megumin said. "Her diligence and stiffness have disappeared, and I think her brain has gone soft. No doubt it's due to your influence, Kazuma."

Darkness flushed bright red to know that I had seen straight through her little abuse of power.

"Both of you, stop it! Darkness is a very dreamy young lady! She says cute clothes and stuffed animals don't suit her, but she loves them both, and when everyone's out of the house, she secretly comes to check on Emperor Zel! She's a very good girl, okay?! Such a sweet, pure young lady is perfectly free to alter her family registry and— Hey, what are you doing, Darkness? I'm trying to help you!"

Darkness, tears in her eyes, had grabbed Aqua in hopes of shutting her mouth.

At that moment, there was a knock on the front door. We heard it click open.

"I'm letting myself in... Sounds like you're all having a good time in here."

Who should appear, smiling at this everyday scene, but Chris.

7

"And that's the story. I've already asked my lowly assistant for help, but if possible, I'd also like all of you to assist me in collecting the Sacred Treasures."

Chris finished her summary of the story so far and let out a breath. The entire time, she had never once taken her eyes off Vanir's shell (aka Zel's bed), which had to be pretty distracting.

Darkness frowned apologetically. "I want to help you, Chris, I really do, but… I'm sorry. With our governor gone to who-knows-where and my father not yet fully recovered, I have to take care of overseeing this town. I'd have to wait until my father is better to help you effectively…"

"No, I understand. That's important work. I'm happy just to know you're on my side. Thank you, Darkness." Chris smiled at her friend, then looked at the other two girls with eyes full of hope.

"If there's something I can help with, then I will," Megumin said. "But I'm not sure there's much I can do. Although, if you find the item has fallen into the hands of some villain, you're welcome to threaten him with an explosion courtesy of yours truly."

"Th-thanks, Megumin. I'll be sure to ask if there's anything I think you can help with. And, uh, that just leaves…"

Chris looked, still hopeful, at Aqua, who was busy fussing over Emperor Zel. Aqua, however, replied bluntly:

"Sorry, I can't help you."

Everyone stared at her. Maybe they hadn't expected that reaction.

"You have nothing to do but feed that chick and lounge around, don't you?" I said. "You've got the most free time out of any of us. You could at least help a little."

Aqua held Emperor Zel close to her chest and gave me a condescending smile. It ticked me off, but if I said something and she started crying and carrying on, this discussion would never get anywhere.

Aqua kept stroking Zel gently—maybe she was enjoying the feel of his fluff—as she said with a self-satisfied look, "Listen, Kazuma. I wonder: Do you understand how a parent really feels?"

"…Why are you asking me that? If I understood that, would my buddies in my online game have nicknamed me Makes-His-Mom-Cry Kazuma?"

"True enough. That's what makes you you, isn't it, Kazuma? A guy who never goes to school, just plays games. When someone tries to get him to go to school, he throws ugly little tantrums… But you know what? Even the most worthless son is precious in the eyes of his parents."

Did she think she was talking about me? Ooh, she was gonna get it…

"I happen to know that you people say a child only gets more beloved the worse he is. But I'm going to make my Zel into the strongest, most venerated, and greatest dragon of all! He's going to learn to be a hero and stand at the zenith of the dragon world… And to that end, your ever-intelligent Aqua has thought of a plan. You know how they say children learn by imitating their parents? I'm going to show Emperor Zel just how strong and worshipped I can be."

All of a sudden, Aqua was looking very serious.

"And how, exactly, are you going to do that?" I asked.

"At first I thought I might try defeating the Demon King, but I figured with my current power, there's an ever-so-slight chance I might fail. So I'll consider that a last resort."

"…I'm sure I have no idea what you're talking about, but didn't you originally buy that chick in the hopes that *he* would fight the Demon King for you? I think you've got your logic backward."

"What *are* you talking about, Kazuma? I could never make my dear, sweet child do such a dangerous thing."

"*You* said it!"

I guess her maternal instincts had hatched along with that egg.

"Anyway, showing him my strong side can wait awhile. There's something more important coming up—a big event."

...A big event?

Aqua looked at each of us in turn.

"You all know the Eris Appreciation Festival?" she asked suddenly.

The Eris Appreciation Festival.

It was a celebration in praise of the goddess of good fortune, Eris, expressing joy and thanks for the safe completion of another year. It was a tradition observed around this time in every corner of this world.

I glanced at Chris, who was sipping tea beside me, and she looked away in embarrassment.

"So you have the Eris Festival in Axel, too?" Megumin asked. "We celebrated it back in our village as well. It's said that if you dress up as Eris, the goddess of good fortune, on that day, you'll be safe all year until the next festival."

Wow. She even managed to inspire a dress code. Impressed, I glanced at Chris, but she gave me a little shake of her head.

Apparently, it was just superstition.

"My family is involved in the Eris Festival every year," Darkness said. "The Dustiness family are all very devout Eris followers. We always make a large donation at the beginning of the festival."

That seemed to embarrass Chris a little.

"So I'll get to see people doing Lady Eris cosplay around here?" I asked. "Hey, that sounds kind of fun!"

"You think so?" Megumin asked. "I am not the biggest fan of that festival myself. It's not only women who dress up as Eris."

"I didn't need to know that."

At that moment, Aqua pounded the table with a *bang*.

"What are you all so excited about?! I didn't bring this up so we could talk about how great the festival was going to be! You're completely leaving me— Ow, ow, ow, ow! Emperor Zel, why are you pecking me?! What is it you don't like about your mother?!"

Aqua's sudden outburst had startled the chick, who pecked at her fingers.

"What are you getting at?" I asked wearily, and Aqua said:

"If there's an Eris Festival, it's only fair that there be an Aqua Festival, too. This year, we're going to cancel the Eris Festival and have an Aqua Festival instead!"

Chris spat out her tea.

Ignoring the choking thief, Aqua went on with increasing volume. "I mean, don't you think it's unfair?! How can they have a festival for Eris without having one for her senior goddess Aqua?! There's no reason they shouldn't let me have a festival once in a while! I want to show Emperor Zel my best side!"

What a thing to say right in front of him.

"Plus, everyone thinks Eris is so great, but you know what? Behind that sweet little face she's got a devil-may-care side to her. And she tends to take things on herself and try her best to do everything alone. I can't even count how many times I've found myself saving that girl's skin; she's just not experienced enough yet!"

Chris was still coughing, and now she was red up to her ears.

"Has she really helped you out that much?" I whispered to her.

"…J-just once. But that was only after I had been super-busy taking care of all this work she had foisted off on me so that my own work just kept piling up… So then when I was having trouble, she was like, 'Sheesh, you're so helpless! Eris, you would be lost without me!' All self-satisfied. But she did help me…"

Puh-leez.

As Chris and I sat whispering, Darkness started in with distinct annoyance. "My goodness, Aqua, it's because you keep bad-mouthing Lady Eris like this that you have such terrible luck. I'm sure all the trouble you keep getting into is divine punishment from Our Lady."

"You must be kidding! So you think that time the stray dog I was teasing suddenly started chasing me or the time I dropped the ice cream I'd just bought were Eris's doing?! For such a pretty face, she must be one mean girl!"

I glanced to my side, where Chris was tearfully shaking her head.

"Well, whatever," Darkness said. "I'm certainly not helping you. Like I said before, I'm very busy as acting governor right now. I don't expect to be able to spare a lot of time during festival season."

"Why not?! And after I helped Kazuma rescue you when you were about to be married off and broke the curse on your father, too!"

"Er... Y-you make a fair point, and it pains me to refuse you, but I am a devout Eris follower..."

That caused Chris to let out a small breath of relief.

"Fine, Darkness, you abandoned divorcée!"

"Abandoned divorcée?! Hold it, Aqua, where'd you learn—?!"

"What about you, Megumin?! Come on, Megumin—how about it? You'll help me, won't you?!"

"Abandoned divorcée..." The abandoned divorcée looked at the floor as if she might cry; meanwhile, Megumin was timidly petting Emperor Zel.

"I don't especially mind," she said. "I'm not an Eris follower in particular, and I do know some Axis disciples. I owe them a very small debt from long ago."

"?!"

That caught Chris's full attention. Aqua looked overjoyed.

"That's my Megumin! And, Kazuma, I know I can count on you."

"The hell you can."

"Help me, you dumb NEET! All you ever do is sleep! Please, I'm asking you—I'll even let you feed Emperor Zel for me! I'll let you do it just once!"

"Not interested! And why are you acting like feeding that chick is some kind of reward anyway?!"

"U-um, I would like to try feeding him...," Megumin said.

Apparently, *some* of us considered it a reward.

"Anyway, canceling the Eris Festival? That's impossible. The Eris Church would have your head on a platter."

"Aww... Doing something about that is your job, my friend Kazuma. You always come up with a plan..."

"Piss off," I said bluntly, and Chris sighed in relief again.

Aqua, however, jumped up and declared, "I've had enough of you, you cheapskate! Megumin and Chris and I will figure out something together—you'll see!"

"Huh?!"

Chris sounded more surprised than anyone had all day.

May There Be a Master for This Sacred Armor!

1

Summer sunlight seeped in between the thick curtains.

I was just pulling the covers up over my head to block out the light when there came a frantic pounding on the door.

"Hey, Kazuma, how long are you going to sleep?! You have clothes on, right? You're not doing anything *weird*, are you? You aren't, are you? I'm coming in! ...What the heck?! It's so cold in here!"

First thing in the morning, and Aqua was already full of it. She started shouting the moment she came into my room.

I stuck my head out from under the covers. "Man, it's too early for this much noise. And shut the door, will you? You'll let the cold out."

"I know we've been through this before, but it's already noon. Seriously, though, why is this room freezing? Are you hiding a wild General Winter in your closet? We've already got Chomusuke and Emperor Zel here, so we don't need any more pets, okay?"

"Why would I keep such an obnoxious thing in my room? Look around. See the buckets in each corner? There's ice in them."

Aqua looked into the buckets with sudden interest. "How'd you get ice in the middle of summer? I want ice, too. It's so hard to sleep sometimes."

"You remember how Wiz was blabbering about buying up all that top-quality manatite? It gave me an idea. I used a portion of my moderate wealth to buy a bunch of cheap manatite, and then I made a ton of ice using Freeze. It may be a summer day, but I can nap under the covers in a nice, cold room. I can't imagine anything more luxurious than this."

Aqua looked at me with the covers up to my neck with a touch of envy. "You, my dear Kazuma, are the smartest person I know when it comes to totally wasting both magic and money... But it does seem like tonight is gonna be another scorcher. Do you think you could make me some ice this evening, too?"

"Sure, I don't mind, but what gives? Weren't you going to go to the Axis Church building today?"

After badgering Chris into helping her yesterday, Aqua had been all excited about going to church today to rally her followers.

"As someone who isn't venerated by *anyone*, Kazuma, you clearly would not understand, but it's a little embarrassing to go to your own followers and tell them you're going to have a festival to praise yourself. I plan to bring someone along who can casually propose the idea to everyone else."

She reached a hand into one of the buckets, stirring the ice with a look of relief.

"Maybe you haven't noticed how single-lady adventurers and the receptionist girls have been oddly attracted to me ever since I came into all that money," I said. "What a weird thing for you of all people to get hung up on anyway. You normally just demand whatever you want without a thought to spare for anyone around you. I told you yesterday: I'm not going to help you. And I don't want anything to do with any Axis disciples. Get Megumin or Darkness to go with you."

"I tried crying to Darkness over and over, but she keeps insisting she's busy being governor. And Megumin said she's going to go see a friend today and doesn't have time to play with me."

As she talked, Aqua hefted the bucket of ice and brought it over toward me...

"Hey, what do you think you're doing with that? I'm not going! I have no desire to go outside in this heat. H-hey, stop that! What do you think you're doing to my bed? I just dried out this futon; don't get it wet again! If you get my bed wet, I swear I'll— Fine! Fine, I'll go with you; just put down the bucket!"

A small building on the outskirts of Axel.

"This is it," Aqua said. "I know it doesn't look like much, but I think that's perfect for expressing the humility of the Axis Church."

"It looks like a strong wind might blow it over," I said.

Aqua and I had arrived at the local Axis Church building. Come to think of it, in all the time I had been living in this town, I had never been here before.

"Hey, who is it who runs this place anyway? We're not going to run into any more crazies, are we? I'm sick of 'characters.' If anyone weird shows up, I'm going home."

"You don't have to worry. All the children of the Axis Church are wonderful people. But I haven't met the head of this particular church yet. I hear someone new took over just recently..."

As she spoke, Aqua put her hand on the door...

"Here, is this all right? Take a good look... Argh, I hope this is the last of these things that you want from me."

...when we heard a man's voice from inside, and we froze.

These things?

"...Indeed. I knew I was right to ask you—this is top class, perfect. Don't worry—I know how to handle it. I won't be in any danger. And it's only for my own personal amusement anyway."

The second voice was that of a woman. Aqua and I looked at each other.

"That's all well and good, then. But don't enjoy it too much. It kills people every year—be careful."

It sounded like we had wandered into the middle of something serious. Surely the Axis Church wasn't involved in the black market, was it...?!

Huh… Actually, it wouldn't be that surprising.

"Hey, Aqua, change of plans. Let's go to the police."

"W-wait just a second! My children would never sully their hands with criminal activity! This has to be some kind of mistake—at least wait until we hear their side of the story!"

"Your little gang of followers sexually harasses Eris disciples and does all sorts of ugly things to them. That's a crime if there ever was one."

Whatever the case, this didn't seem like a good place to be. If the people inside knew we had overheard them, they might try to silence us with extreme prejudice.

I was just about to drag the uncooperative Aqua off by force when—

"Goodness, you have not changed a bit. Are you that fond of this white powder?"

That was Megumin's voice.

Aqua and I were shocked to suddenly hear one of our friends. What was Megumin doing in there? And had she just said something about white powder?

Wait a second, if Megumin is part of such underhanded dealings, then…

"Is this really such good stuff?" Megumin's voice went on. "You recommended it to me as well once, and I've developed an interest in it."

Hold up.

"Listen, lady, this may look like just white powder at first glance. But when you dissolve it in warm water…"

No, wait, stop.

I mean, we're sure that's Megumin in there, right? Not someone else who just happens to sound like her?

Aqua and I were trying to decide whether to charge in there when we heard something we couldn't ignore.

"If you're curious, why not try it? It's okay, Miss Megumin; everyone's scared the first time. But once you've experienced it, I'm sure you won't be able to stop…"

I kicked open the door.

2

"—Hold it right there, you degenerate disciples!! I don't know what you're doing to my friend, but I'm gonna rip you a new one!"

Inside was a man and a woman, both utterly shocked to see the door fly open. And—

"K-Kazuma?! Why are you here…?! And Aqua too…?!"

—between them was Megumin, looking equally surprised.

"Forget why I'm here! Hey, you criminals, don't move a muscle! I know I'm not much to look at, but I'm actually a famous adventurer around here, and if you try to resist, I'll show you what I'm really made of!"

My threat caused the woman—she looked like an Axis priestess—to tremble with the white powder in her hand. "W-wait! Yes, this is contraband, but I was the only one who was going to use it, so—"

"As if I'd believe that! I just heard you offering some to my companion! Don't play with me—what am I going to do if my friend gets any crazier than she already is?! I'm going to burn that awful stuff up with Kindle!"

As I spoke, I held out my right hand; the priestess discreetly stuffed the powder back into a bag.

Aqua rushed past me, shouting, "*God Blow*!!"

And slammed her fist into the man, who hadn't really been following what was going on.

It caught him square in the solar plexus, and he crumpled to the ground without even a squeak.

"Hey, what do you two think you're doing?!" Megumin yelped. "Barging in here and—and causing chaos?!"

I ignored her, facing the priestess with my fists raised. "Quiet, Megumin! Now listen to me, you crappy cleric! Where do you get off leading an innocent young girl down the path of evil?! I'm all about true gender equality—I don't care if you're a priest *and* a woman; I'll still beat the crap out of you. You'll pay for getting my friend involved in this awful stuff. Your goddess might not be willing to raise her followers right, but my 'holy fist' should be plenty for you."

Aqua grabbed hold of my arm to keep me from decking the priestess right then and there. "Hey, Kazuma, don't jump to conclusions! I'm sure this young lady can offer some explanation! This guy here doesn't look like an Axis disciple, so I was more than willing to pass judgment on him, but I can detect the aura of a pious Axis follower from this girl! Wait until we've heard what she has to say!"

The priestess looked at Aqua, her eyes going wide. "Who are—?! …Ah, well, look at that… Heh-heh, I can't do anything bad. Very well, I lose. Burn this stuff and hand me over to the police…" No sooner had she looked at Aqua than her shoulders went limp and she confessed her crime.

"M-miss?!" Next to her, Megumin looked from me to the priestess and back, still totally confused.

"If you're not going to resist, then we won't hurt you," I said. "But we will need you to come with us to the police. You can make restitution for your crime there."

"Yes, I understand… Heh-heh— Miss Megumin, do you think you can still regard me so politely after seeing me this way? You needn't look so worried. After I've paid for my crime, I'm sure we'll see each other again… By evening today, if I had to guess…"

A fleeting smile passed over her face.

"…Evening today? What do you mean? You're going away for a lot longer than that."

"What do *you* mean? Illegal possession of gelatinous slime is mostly punishable by a short lecture."

Gelatinous slime.

"…What exactly does that slime do? Do you become an addict if you use it or turn to ash or—"

"Nothing of the sort," Megumin said. "Why would you ever imagine such terrible things would happen? Gelatinous slime is popular with old people and children because of how pleasant it is going down and the kind of wobbly quality it imparts to food."

That caused me to shut my mouth.

"……Okay, hold on, but wait. Earlier, that guy was saying people die every year from it…"

"A lot of people wolf it down without chewing thoroughly, and it gets stuck in their throat, choking them to death. Did you know it's a popular gift for young wives to give their mothers-in-law on their birthdays?"

……

"W-wait, okay. You guys said this stuff was illegal, and it's a white powder and everything. So having it is a crime, right?"

The priestess shook her head with a sad expression. "There was an incident in Arcanletia in which the Demon King's army used gelatinous slime in an indiscriminate terror attack… It was terrible; every bath in town was turned into gelatinous slime. Ever since then, people have been researching this stuff, convinced that if the Demon King's army used it, there must have been some reason—some nefarious side effect. Questions of safety have led to recommendations not to eat it…"

Why would the Demon King's army do a stupid thing like that?

"But for me, there's no substitute for gelatinous slime! So even though I know people will scold me for it, I just can't stop…!"

The priestess burst into tears. Personally, I was starting to think it was time to head home.

"O pious Axis follower," Aqua said, placing her hand on the priestess's shoulder. "Remember thou the seventh of the Axis precepts."

The priestess looked up at her. "The seventh precept…? …! 'Follower, do not practice self-denial. Drink when you wish to drink; eat when you wish to eat. You never know if that dish will still be available tomorrow…'"

"Exactly. Do not practice self-denial. Be it the fried chicken on someone else's plate, if you wish to eat it, then eat it. If you want to eat gelatinous slime, you must not deny yourself. Self-denial is like poison to the body."

"Ahh… Lady Aqua, thank you…!!"

I took a few steps back from Aqua and the priestess and their weird thing going on, and I whispered to Megumin, who had come up beside me, "Hey, what's with these two? Should we stop them? Or should we just quietly walk away?"

"If I had to choose, I should certainly think the latter, but I believe this will all blow over shortly," she said. "But more importantly, why are you both here? Aqua told me this morning there was somewhere she wanted me to go with her—is this the place she was talking about?"

3

We tended to the collapsed merchant, then saw him off. Ignoring the weird little ongoing drama between Aqua and the priestess, I brought Megumin up to speed.

"…And that is why you thought these people were about to get me involved in something terrible and came bursting through the door?"

"Yeah, exactly. Sorry, though. That priestess is an acquaintance of yours, right? I think, uh, our misunderstanding caused her a lot of trouble."

I scratched my cheek apologetically, but Megumin just giggled. "It's okay. It shows how much you care, right? 'Hold it right there, you degenerate disciples!! I don't know what you're doing to my friend, but I'm gonna rip you a new one!'—wasn't that what you said? Heh, yet another memorable Kazuma-ism."

"St-stoppit; forget it already. I was really desperate when I said that… Hey, stop grinning; I'll grab you by those grinning cheeks."

Even my attempts at intimidation didn't stop Megumin from smiling.

...But it was a relief to know we'd made a fuss over nothing...

"Aaaahhhh!"

Suddenly, a mood-killing groan echoed through the church. It came from the priestess Aqua had been comforting until just then.

"What the hell is that—?! What's *with* this guy?! Miss Megumin smiles at him and he just pretends he doesn't like it *that* much, like a total *tsundere*! And you, Miss Megumin, you look totally ridiculous, teasing to hide your affection! Ahhh, Miss Megumin, you're so adorable! Can I give you a big hug?! Just one!"

"St-stop that, please. Ahem, I haven't introduced you three yet, have I?" Megumin backed away from the arm-flailing priestess and turned to us. "Kazuma, Aqua, allow me to introduce Miss Cecily. She's the head of this church. Er, she's my..."

"Big sister."

"Please do not lie so readily! She, um, has been very helpful to me in the past..."

I wondered what the story was with this Cecily woman. She was very attractive, but I sensed the same good-for-nothing aura from her that I did from all my party members.

At length, Cecily turned to Aqua and bowed her head. "Please allow me to introduce myself properly... Lady Aqua, whom I have the pleasure of meeting for the very first time. Father Zesta, the highest-ranking person in the church hierarchy, informed us about you. My name is Cecily. If there is anything I can do for you, please ask, whatever it may be." Then she gave Aqua the sort of smile you normally reserved for the person you loved most in the world.

"Ooh, *anything*, you say? So if I said my socks have holes in them and I want you to buy me some new ones, you would do it?"

"Of course, Lady Aqua! I would even remove your honorable socks for you if you wished... Hey! What do you think you're doing? You can't grab a girl just because she's pretty!"

I was pulling the jabbering Cecily over to one corner of the church.

"Look, don't let her walk all over you," I said. "It'll just go to her head. Say... You're awfully subservient for someone meeting Aqua for the first time. Don't tell me... Has the Axis Church caught on to who she really is?"

"I'm afraid I don't know what you're talking about. Lady Aqua is Lady Aqua. That person is the Arch-priest who saved our town. And *just* an Arch-priest, even though she has the same name as Our Lady. I came to this town as a servant of that Lady Aqua, in order to glorify her even with my eating and sleeping."

"Maybe you could do us a favor and go back to Arcanletia."

Still, her reaction shed some light on the situation. It seemed likely that the Axis Church had finally figured out who Aqua really was, and that rather than publicly celebrating her advent, they had decided to just quietly keep an eye on her.

At the very least, it didn't look like Cecily had any intention of doing Aqua or me any harm.

...Then suddenly, Aqua, who had sidled up to me in the meantime, tugged on my sleeve. She kept glancing at me like she was eager to say something. I guessed this was the part where she wanted me to suggest holding an Aqua Festival because she was too embarrassed to say it herself. What a pain.

"So, uh, you're Megumin's acquaintance Cecily, right?"

"Yes, but you don't have to refer to me so elaborately. You're welcome to just call me Big Sis Cecily."

Geez. It suddenly felt like there was a second Aqua in the room.

Beside me, the first Aqua was blinking rapidly as if to say, *Quick, hurry up!* Sheesh.

"Er... Uh, you know the Eris Appreciation Festival is happening in this town pretty soon, right?"

"Yes! You're damn right I know! I'm well aware of those despicable Eris followers and their stupid festival that celebrates Eris without even acknowledging Our Lady Aqua!" Cecily took the bait and was off and running. "They do it in the summer. Well, what do you associate with summer? That's right: the beach, the pool, and the Axis Church. And what do you associate with festivals? The Axis Church, obviously. We love parties and celebrations, and we especially love summer, and they choose this exact season to celebrate Eris and leave us out entirely! They're practically begging for a fight. Even war! This means war!"

Is this the only kind of person in the Axis Church?

As for Aqua, Cecily's little speech had caused her eyes to start glimmering.

"So here's what we're gonna do," Cecily went on. "Right this minute, I'm gonna go over to the Eris Church and smash their windows. They'll get so angry, they'll chase me back this way; then Megumin will make a dramatic entrance, give one of her cool introductions, and kick all their asses! Your job is to hide among the onlookers and mutter something pompous like 'Looks like those evil Eris disciples have gotten their divine punishment...' And as for you, Lady Aqua, you can just stay here, lounging about and drinking wine or something... All right, here we go!"

"Yeah... You're not going anywhere. Pointing out the negative aspects of that plan would be like shooting fish in a barrel! ...And, you two, stop looking so eager!"

Megumin was grinning over her given responsibility, while Aqua was all too happy to do her "job." I ignored them both; I had to do something about this Axis follower.

"That's not what I had in mind. I was thinking, you know, some kind of competing Aqua Appreciation Festival."

4

"Hello, everyone. My name is Cecily, and I'm the head of the Axis Church in Axel Town. I have a request I'd like to make of you all."

"Please go home."

We were in Axel's downtown district. There, every owner of every shop was busy getting ready for the Eris Appreciation Festival.

"What?! After I came here and asked you so nicely?! …Aha, I see you're trying to take advantage of this situation. I know just what you'll say! 'Hoo-hoo-hoo, oh, Miss Beautiful Axis Priestess, if you want us to listen to you, first show us how sincere you are!' And then you'll take my generous body, and…! Well, I won't let you get away with this, you heathens! I'll show you the power of an Axis disciple!"

"Watch out—this girl is crazy! This is why no one wants anything to do with Axis followers— Stop, hold on! Somebody help!"

Before my very eyes, Cecily was strangling the man who served as the president of the downtown district.

"…Hey, Megumin, you're her friend, aren't you? Go stop her."

"We're not friends; we are acquaintances. Please do not be confused on that point."

We'd come here only to get permission for our festival. Why did just having an Axis follower around always lead to a fight?

I'd left Aqua at the church on the assumption that having two problem children along would keep the discussion from going anywhere, but it looked like one wasn't much better.

Megumin and I looked around the shopping district again. Staff at the various shops were busy preparing the goods they wanted to sell at the festival, as well as making what appeared to be streamers.

The scene really brought back memories of Japanese culture festivals. I had been sent to this world just after my own culture festival concluded. I ended up not going to school on the day of, but if I had known I was going to end up in another world, maybe I would have.

I think my class had decided to do a fried-noodle stand.

I looked back at Cecily, who was still busy upbraiding the president.

…Sure, they were Axis followers, but they just wanted to have a celebration.

Thinking about Japan had made me a little sentimental, and I went over to try to stop Cecily from choking the guy to death.

I had originally just kind of been dragged along here, but seeing all this gave me a very slight change of heart.

"Okay, Cecily, that's enough of that. It's not getting us anywhere. Let me talk to him."

Cecily's hands relaxed on the man's windpipe. Through a fit of coughing, the president said, "I don't care who talks to me or what they say; we won't— Hmm? Are you perchance Mr. Satou, the exceedingly rich adventurer?"

What was that, a new nickname? I mean, not that it wasn't appropriate.

Cecily seemed to calm down now that the president looked ready to talk; she straightened her disheveled clothes, clasped her hands as if in prayer, and gave the man a beseeching look.

"We were thinking," she said, "about the annual Eris Appreciation Festival. We would like it to be changed to an Aqua Appreciation Festival—"

"Go home."

"...! ...!!"

"You're just going to get in the way! Come over here with me, Sis," Megumin said, dragging Cecily off before she could attack the president again.

He looked thoroughly intimidated as I whispered to him, "I'm really sorry about the trouble my companion is causing... Although we did come here in connection with what she's talking about."

"You mean the Aqua Appreciation Festival that insane Axis girl mentioned? Impossible—what do you suppose the Eris followers would think about a decision like that?"

I could see he wasn't biting. I continued whispering. "No, no, we won't ask you to do anything as outrageous as changing the festival—no matter what she says. We just want the two festivals to run in tandem. Call it the Eris and Aqua Appreciation Festival, and we'll be happy."

The president didn't look entirely convinced. "You know I can't approve such a thing. I can't see any benefit to it, and I see a lot of potential to cause trouble…"

"I know the Eris Appreciation Festival needs the cooperation of everyone in the merchants' quarter," I commented, as if the idea had just occurred to me, "and it makes a fair amount of money each year, doesn't it?" I spoke as casually as I could.

"Well, I would be lying if I said we didn't see a certain amount of profit. But over the last several years, increased activity from the Demon King's army has caused us to come up a little short… What's your point?"

Ah yes, indeed.

"Eris followers and Axis followers," I said. "I know they don't usually get along. But even so, the Axis Church is just showing their veneration… Now, what if they were to work together to make this festival happen? That Axis brigade loves a celebration, and I'm sure they'd come up with something big. And I can't think the Eris Church would let themselves be outdone."

"…Tell me more," the president said, leaning in.

"We pit them against each other. Fan their mutual hostility to make this festival bigger and bigger. And of course, a rising tide lifts all boats."

The president rubbed his chin thoughtfully, looking serious. But I wasn't done enumerating the advantages.

"…There's one more thing. Where does the funding for the festival come from each year?"

"The funding? The Eris Church covers the majority of it, with the nobles and us merchants making up the difference…"

I leaned in like the president was doing and said, "If the Axis Church is so eager to participate, why not get them to contribute, too? The two religious organizations between them could fund the entire cost of the festival."

"…Yes, let's do it; let's absolutely do it! Ah, now I see how someone as young as you got so rich, Mr. Satou. I would love to ask you to be the adviser for this festival. Not for free, of course…"

Ooh, I hadn't been expecting that.

I wasn't exactly hurting for money, but I wasn't going to pass up such a tasty opportunity.

"I would love to, if you'll have me. I'll give you my best ideas—now let's go make some easy money."

"Ah, what a wonderful proposition you've brought me!"

We started laughing so suddenly that people turned to look at us. Somewhere in the background, I heard two voices whispering:

"Should we really be trusting him to handle this?"

"Even your 'big sister' is starting to feel a little anxious."

5

At the café that had quickly become my customary meeting spot with Chris, I reported to the thief everything that had happened.

"—And so that's what we're going to do."

"But whyyyyyy?! *Why* is that what you're going to do?! I figured there was no way—how did my senior ever manage to convince the president of the shopping district to go along with this?!" Chris pounded the table, her voice loud enough to be heard all over the café.

"Oh yeah, I had to work pretty hard to persuade him. But in the end, he was happy to do it."

"*You* persuaded him?!"

I had my arms crossed and was nodding in appreciation of my own fine work; in contrast, Chris was weeping openly and very upset.

"Why?! I know how much you hate having to put yourself out even the tiniest bit, so why would you get us into something as convoluted as this? The way things are going, I'll have to forgo my own celebration to help with my senior's festival. That's the stupidest thing I've ever heard!"

"L-listen, why *should* you have to help? We can just say you're backing out."

Chris had her head in her hands. "We can try, but… Somehow, when she asks me to do something, I always find myself pressured into it… Like the way I'm always expected to resurrect you these days…"

"Er, and I'm, uh, very grateful for that, by the way… Anyway, just calm down. I swear there's a good reason for all this."

I explained to the still-thoroughly-agitated Chris what I had discussed with the president, leaving out the parts about my being an adviser and there being an honorarium.

"You see, all this anxiety over the Demon King's army has made it hard for people to get excited for anything, even a festival. So I wondered what would happen if we brought in the Axis Church, which seems to love throwing parties. I hoped we could bring everyone just a moment's relief from their fear, a chance to forget what was upsetting them."

"I guess I can't really object when you put it like that, but…when did you start caring so much about the well-being of the townspeople?"

"Goodness, what a thing to say to someone who's defeated so many powerful enemies and even helped find a Sacred Treasure—I'm full of good deeds."

"S-sorry! That's not what I…! Okay, I get it. Maybe I can play along. I don't think my senior will go for anything all that crazy anyway… Will she?"

"……So, uh, the whole cohosting thing is just an idea for this year. Knowing Aqua, she'll probably be happy to do it this once, and next year everything can go back to normal."

"Hey, why aren't you reassuring me about her craziness?! Is—is this gonna be okay…? And you said the Axis Church is better at parties. My festival isn't gonna disappear next year, is it…? I—I mean, not that I'm begging to be celebrated, all right?"

I understood that she was concerned about the future of her festival, but Chris was starting to sound almost as annoying as Aqua. Maybe all goddesses were this way.

"Well, let's table that for now. Have you found out where the Sacred Treasure is?"

"Yeah, I've pinpointed the location. The only problem is, it's a little dangerous. A noble named Undyne has it, but he's got a reputation for collecting...weird things."

A noble who collected bizarre artifacts.

Based on my experiences so far, I got the impression the nobility was composed entirely of freaks and weirdos.

"If it's a noble we're dealing with, why not ask Darkness for help? She could pressure him to give the item to her family..."

"That would never work. It sounds like Undyne obtained this item illegally, and I'm sure he'd play dumb. Among the nobility, he's notorious for doing anything he has to in order to get what he wants. Even if Darkness tried to negotiate with him, I'm sure he would claim he didn't know what she was talking about, and that would be the end of it."

My impression of nobles just kept getting better and better.

Illegally? So maybe he stole it or maybe threatened someone into giving it to him.

The upside was, that meant a more nefarious means of getting the item back was open to us.

"I think I know what this means, Chief."

"I think you do, Lowly Assistant."

It was time to put on the mask again.

6

I had a quick look at Undyne's mansion, and on the way home, I mulled over how to break in to it.

Aqua had gotten back before me, and when I arrived, I found her making a commotion. She was pounding on the door of the first-floor toilet.

"Come on, Darkness! Please? When Kazuma gets home, I'll help you yell at him! Please come out of the bathroom already! We can't afford to let you shut yourself up in there! The toilet on the second floor is backed up—*somebody* didn't clean it! Please come out of there! Come on, hurry!"

Apparently, Darkness was holed up inside.

"I'm back. Hey, what's all this about? What are you going to yell at me for when I get home?"

I saw Megumin slumped on the living room sofa; she must have gotten Aqua to take her out for her daily explosion.

"Listen to me, you dumb NEET! Darkness came home practically crying because you've been spreading embarrassing secrets about her everywhere! 'Miss Lalatina, is it true your abs are ripped?' they ask! 'Miss Lalatina, is it true your brand-new husband ran out on you?' 'Miss Lalatina, you're so pretty; I'm sure even as an abandoned divorcée, you'll find somebody.' Every adventurer she meets teases her! Come on, Darkness—come on out! I'm sure you of all people will find another husband soon! I promise not to call you Divorce-ness anymore! Just please, please be happy again!"

Was Aqua trying to get Darkness to come out of the bathroom or stay in there? She was so dense; I couldn't tell.

"Hey, Darkness," I interrupted, "you're gonna be in everyone's way there, so come on out. Anyway, remember that when I broke into the Dustiness mansion and told you I was going to spread your embarrassing secrets around, you're the one who said to do whatever. But look, I really am sorry, Lalatina."

There was a *slam* against the bathroom door. Apparently, Lalatina had given up crying and was now feeling very angry.

She didn't respond to Aqua's wheedling and wouldn't answer anything I said, either.

It really was going to be a problem to have our only bathroom constantly occupied.

"Look, I was wrong there, but so were you. I may have been looking

for trouble, but you gave it to me. I apologize, so let's bury the hatchet…
I can pee while standing, so it doesn't make much difference to me, but
if you don't come out soon, I think Aqua might not make it, so hurry up
and be nice again."

"I told you: Goddesses don't use the bathroom, so I absolutely will
'make it'!" Aqua shouted, fidgeting. "It's just that I'm responsible for cleaning the downstairs toilet! If Darkness doesn't come out, I won't be able to
do my job! There's absolutely no other reason for this! So come on out!"

Much as I wanted to enjoy putting the screws to Aqua at that
moment, cleaning the upstairs toilet was, as I recalled, my responsibility. I would hate for Aqua to point that out, so instead I made one final
appeal to Darkness.

"Listen up, Darkness. We've been around each other long enough
for you to know me pretty well. If you really insist on not leaving the
bathroom, believe me, this will end with you crying and apologizing
and begging me to stop."

The immediate response to my words was a derisive snort from
inside the bathroom. Then Darkness finally broke her silence and
said, "You've known *me* long enough to know that I can turn even the
worst experiences into pleasure. What, are you going to resort to your
specialty—saying mean things about me? I'm holding your bathroom
hostage. I can just plug my ears and ignore whatever you say, so you're
the one at a disadvantage here. House Dustiness outdoes all other fami-
lies when it comes to endurance… Let's go, then—let's see who can last
longer! Today is the day I stay in here until you call me Lady Dustiness
and cry for me to forgive you!"

………

At that, I went over to the heavy table in the middle of the living
room and dragged it over so it was in front of the bathroom door.

The bathroom was in a hallway right outside the living room. The
table was just about as wide as that hallway, so by pulling it over there, I
effectively blocked the bathroom door.

I whispered something to Aqua, then walked away.

Aqua watched me go, then turned to the door and announced, "Hey, Darkness. Kazuma said he's headed to your room, and he's going to pull everything out of the chests and closet and out from under the bed, and he's going to *enjoy* himself as much as he wants. And then he just…walked off."

There was a huge crash from the bathroom. Next came the smack of the door hitting the table as Darkness tried to get out.

I completely ignored both noises as I headed up the stairs…

I heard the door hit the table several more times, and then Darkness was shouting. "Kazumaaa! Stop it! Stop, you fiend! Cease! Desist! St—! This is a joke, isn't it? Aqua, Kazuma's still there, isn't he? Megumin, is Kazuma still there?!"

Her voice got more and more frantic and weepy.

To make things worse, Megumin, from where she sat on the sofa, listlessly petting Emperor Zel (still sleeping in the arms of Vanir's empty shell), joined Aqua in saying:

""No, he's not.""

"Kazuma, I was wrong! I was…! Hey, let me out; I can't get out of here! Aqua, Megumin, let me out! Kazuma, I was wrong; I'm sorry! I'm so sorry! Please forgive me, Lord Kazuma!"

A little while later.

"…Ergh, my favorite underwear…"

"…Um, what happened to Darkness after that?" Megumin inquired. We were all sitting at the table, discussing what we would do next over dinner.

"If you want to know, ask her. Aqua, what happened after we left? I helped get permission for your festival. Will you be able to handle the rest on your own?"

"Sure. Now that we've been approved, everything else should be fine. Just leave it all to me—I have an idea."

Having wrangled permission from the shopping district president, I was going to leave everything else entirely in Aqua's hands. I would be lying if I said that didn't worry me a little, but hey, I wasn't an Axis disciple, so there was really no further reason for me to be involved.

It was my hope that the Eris and Axis Churches would get competitive and make the celebration bigger and bigger. I would do my part to fan the flames but otherwise leave them to celebrate however they liked.

Fight... Then fight some more...!

"Hey, Kazuma," Darkness said. "What exactly does permission for this festival entail?"

"Figh— Oh! I mean, the president of the shopping district, you know? He decided to let the Eris and Axis Churches cohost the festival so that it would be bigger than ever."

"You really got him to agree to that? I can't imagine how... Wait, yes I can. Knowing you, it was probably something I don't want to hear about. Argh, why does this have to happen when I'm the acting governor...?" Darkness heaved a sigh and had a bite of pasta. "Mm," she said, "this pasta is good. In fact, all the food tonight is tasty. It doesn't quite compare to the chefs at my family's house, but I wouldn't turn up my nose at this at a restaurant. Who did the cooking today?"

"I did," I said. "...Oh, I get it; you ran out on us during the incident with that lord, so you don't know. I picked up the Cooking skill. I've got all that money, and I'm thinking about how to live the good life, see? So I thought, rather than focus on skills that would help with adventuring, why not pick up some things that could enrich my daily life?"

Darkness put her head in her hands. "Wh-why, you... I've had a bad feeling about you ever since you took the Flee skill. I wondered where you were headed with all this... The Cooking skill is normally reserved for chefs!"

Yeah, but still.

7

After that, Aqua started going to the Axis Church on a daily basis, leaving our lives largely peaceful.

But one night...

It was well past midnight, so late that dawn would be coming in just a few hours.

Chris and I stood outside our target, the Undyne house.

"Why did you pick so late at night, Lowly Assistant? We could have started the operation a little earlier, couldn't we?"

"Humans sleep more deeply at this time of night. Right after they fall asleep, the tiniest noise can wake them up. When I was living with my family in Japan, I learned this was the best time to sneak to the kitchen for a snack. I'm using hard-won wisdom from my own life here."

We were no longer Kazuma Satou and Chris; we had become the Lowly Assistant and Chief of the Silver-Haired Thief Brigade.

I had my mask on again, and I was dressed all in black and carrying a big bag.

Happily, it was cloudy that night. With no light from the moon or stars, everything around us was pitch-black.

"Fine, I won't bug you about it... Hey, what's with the big bag? What's wrapped up in that cloth?"

Chris seemed to have taken an interest in my baggage.

I was carrying soundproof materials for absorbing impacts. It was a type of homemade Bubble Wrap I'd been working on. My first proto-type had been used as a stress reliever by a certain crazy someone, but I had gone on to make second and third prototypes.

We were going to be stealing armor, after all. If we tried to just carry it off, it would probably *clank, clank, clank* enough to wake up the whole house.

Chris listened to my explanation with considerable admiration. "Now I get it... Say, Lowly Assistant, you had Bubble Wrap in Japan, right? It's supposed to be fun to pop the bubbles... Can I see that for a second...?"

"I'm not letting you pop these; it takes forever to make this thing. Come on—let's get going."

                              *   *   *

Under the cover of night, we made our way toward the mansion.

Honestly, this particular hit wasn't going to be very difficult. It was nothing compared to infiltrating the royal castle, and although Undyne was a noble, his mansion was nowhere near as large as Darkness's.

There were no guards patrolling outside, and it wasn't even clear if there was anyone keeping watch indoors. I was making full use of the fact that Second Sight allowed me to see in the dark as I pressed myself to the wall of the complex.

"You know, Chief, I've been wondering. You're a goddess. Can't you see in the dark like Aqua?"

"This body is my temporary form on this plane. I haven't incarnated myself directly like my senior did, so I can't see through demons and undead, and I can't detect evil. But on the other hand, I don't radiate a goddess's aura, so undead don't bother me."

That made sense. Attracting zombies would be the last thing you would want at a time like this.

"Okay then, Chief, give me your hand. I'll guide you."

"I don't need to hold your hand to know where to go, Lowly Assistant. When we broke into the castle, I followed you just fine."

"That was completely different. There was moonlight and everything, but tonight there isn't a star in the cloudy sky. One careless moment could cost you your life. Don't underestimate this job just because it's easier than getting into the castle. Come on. Give me your—"

"Kazuma Satou, sexually harassing me will result in severe divine punishment, got it? Like, you'll suddenly feel really sick to your stomach, but when you run to the bathroom, you'll find out someone else is in there. And then, just when you think you've finally made it, you'll discover there's no toilet paper."

"I'm sorry—I got carried away. Please forgive me."

Unlike Aqua's weirdly vague divine punishments, Eris had some very unpleasant wrath in store.

Trembling slightly, I followed along the wall until we got to the back entrance of the house.

"Let's not worry too much tonight. There were no guards, and with our Detect Trap and Lockpick skills, we'll manage somehow. The real issue is after we get the armor. I'm not sure how much my invention will dampen the sound..."

"Let's trust your work, Lowly Assistant. And if push comes to shove, we can always force our way out like we did at the castle!"

Chris seemed to be downright enjoying herself as she unlocked the gate. Thinking back on it, I guess that was kind of fun.

And rife with tension, for some reason.

"You know, that mask of yours really is cool, Lowly Assistant. You said you bought it at the magic-item shop in town, right? And I think that weird doll on your couch was wearing something similar. When this job is over, you'll have to show me where you bought it."

"Sure, but... You're not going to get into a fight with the staff, Chief? Aqua and the part-timer at that place really don't get along. It's a battle every time they see each other."

"I'm not going to fight anyone. That senior of mine, she'll argue with anybody she lays eyes on..."

Come to think of it, Chris had mentioned that this was a temporary body for her—I wondered if Vanir would be able to figure out her true identity. It seemed like Chris couldn't use her goddess powers in this form, and there was actually a chance he wouldn't sense anything from her.

...No. If her identity just happened to get out and it turned into a huge battle, that would be a problem. Maybe it was best not to let them meet...

"There, it's open. Let's get to work, Lowly Assistant."

8

Just as we'd guessed, there were no guards in Undyne's mansion. Maybe it had something to do with the crime rate being relatively low in this town.

I worked my way down the lightless hallway. Chris was using her Sense Treasure skill, and we were heading toward whatever was setting it off, but...

"Chief, you don't have to stop in front of every single piece of loot. Let's just find the Sacred Treasure, go home, and get some sleep."

"Y-yeah, sure, that's what I want, too. It's just, every time I see treasure, it stirs the Thief blood in me... When I think of all the poor children I could help with even one item, my hand just..."

Chris seemed drawn to every painting and exquisite item we passed.

"Do your Robin Hood thing on your own time. Anyway, if you have to steal something, there's probably stuff in the treasure vault that's a lot more valuable—and smaller."

"Yeah, I guess so. It looks like you've started to learn a thing or two about thieving in spite of yourself, Lowly Assistant... Aren't you about at the point where you have enough levels to change jobs? Why not re-class from Adventurer to Thief?"

"I have every intention of living a dissolute life of pleasure, so I'm fine as an Adventurer. We're weak, but we can learn a lot of skills. I'm thinking I'll get Create Earth Golem next. Then maybe I can make a golem to do my chores."

"...You sure love to waste your magic and skills. If I may offer a goddess's perspective, in view of your eventual confrontation with the Demon King, you might want to go for something a little more useful..."

What a thing to say to the guy who'd died more times than anyone else in this world.

We moved on, following Chris's Sense Treasure, until finally we arrived at a room with a thick door. That was when I got a reaction from a skill I was happy to have but that I didn't normally have a use for: Detect Trap.

"I guess you can't blame them for having one trap," Chris said. "Let's see... Ooh, an alarm... Say, Lowly Assistant..."

"I'm a lot of things, but I'm not stupid," I said. "I promise what happened when we broke into the castle won't happen here... S-seriously, I mean it. Stop looking at me like that..."

While Chris disabled the trap, I used my Sense Foe skill, just to make sure we hadn't woken anyone up in the meantime.

"......?"

It wasn't an enemy.

No, not an enemy, but I did feel a strange aura from inside the treasure room. It wasn't human, but it wasn't a monster, either.

"There, got it! Lock's picked, Lowly Assistant!" Chris said, and she put a hand to the door.

"Hey, w-wait just a second, Chief; there's—"

But before I could tell her about the mysterious aura, the door was open.

"...? What's wrong, Lowly Assistant?"

"Huh?"

Inside the vault was...no one.

It couldn't have been my imagination; I could still detect the aura nearby. But the only thing there was a huge pile of weird items...

"Assistant! Lowly Assistant! Look at this! I'll bet this is worth plenty!"

"Aww, no fair! I had my eye on that!" I forgot all about the aura and became completely enamored with the treasure.

"Just to be clear," Chris said, "you have to donate the full amount you get from any treasure you steal, okay? We may be stealing from a villain, but we're not doing it for prof—"

"Hoo, look at this thing sparkle! This looks *wicked* expensive! Ooh, what's this weird stone? Aqua loves weird stones; maybe I should bring it back for her."

"...Ahem. Lowly Assistant? Are you listening? That's off-limits, okay? For real. You hear me?"

That was when I noticed: For all the gold in this room, the crucial suit of armor was missing.

"Chief, I don't see that Sacred Treasure or whatever."

"What?! Dang, you're right. So why does this place give off a divine-level-treasure aura?"

Still a little bugged about the aura I'd felt earlier, I looked in the direction it was coming from. There was a wall there and nothing especially out of the ordinary or...

"Wha—?!"

As I ran my fingers along the wall, part of it suddenly recessed and then spun around, like a rotating wall at a ninja hideout.

"A hidden door? Way to go, Lowly Assistant."

"I may not look like much, but I'm confident I have the next best luck to you, Chief."

Just a little banter as we entered the room beyond the wall.

Smack in the middle of the room stood a suit of armor, bound hand and foot with chains as if to hold it in place.

Made entirely of silver, it looked like a work of art. There wasn't a single seam on the whole smooth surface of the suit. I wasn't exactly an expert appraiser of armor, but somehow as I looked at it, my heart started to pound, and I was overcome with the confidence that if I could just wear this suit of armor, no one could beat me.

"It's...," I breathed.

"Uh-huh. Aigis, the holy armor... It's the toughest armor in this world, granting victory to anyone who wears it."

We approached the chained-up armor for a closer look.

"Hey, it's got some scratches on it," I said.

Chris placed a reverent hand on the armor. "...Yeah, so it does. I guess because it spent all that time protecting its master from the Demon King's army. The owner of this armor never lost a fight, no matter how brutal, to the bitter end." She seemed to be inspecting each of the little marks and scratches. "To the day your owner died of illness, you did your job..."

She accompanied her murmur with a gentle touch of the armor.

Wow, this is the sort of thing that makes her seem really goddess-like…
I was admiring Chris's face in profile when it happened.

<Hey, kiddo, hands off the merchandise!>

A man's voice reverberated in my mind, shattering the solemn atmosphere.

It looked like Chris could hear it, too.

"Huh? K-kiddo? Are you talking about me?! Okay, wait—hang on a second! Was that…*you* talking just now?! You, the sacred armor Aigis?!"

<Huh, so you're not a boy. In that case, go ahead and touch me a little more. Let me start over from the top. A pleasure to meet you both. My name is Sacred Armor Aigis. I'm a sort of hybrid Sacred Treasure that can both speak and sing. You're welcome to call me Mr. Aigis.>

Hey, since when did Sacred Treasures speak so fluently?

Was this what I had felt with my Sense Foe skill?

"Oh, uh…I'm just a little surprised," Chris said. "None of my information said you could talk. So, uh, Aigis."

<I believe I said *Mr.* Aigis, punk.>

"I'm not a punk! Why's a Sacred Treasure like you got such a bad attitude anyway?"

"Chief, let me remind you we've broken in here in the middle of the night, and now is not the time to be arguing with an inanimate object! Remember what we're here for!"

The argument with the armor had advanced so far that Chris was pounding it on the chest (gently), but I pulled the load off my back to remind her of our original objective.

Chris's face turned serious, and she set her hand on the chest plate of the armor.

"…That's right. Okay, er…*Mr.*…Aigis. We broke in here because your power is needed once again. I'll find you a new owner. They'll be an outworlder, just like your last master. Someone who'll come here from a land called Japan to save this world!"

Then she smiled as if to encourage the armor...

<Huh? What're you going on about? Why should I have to do that at this stage in the game? Count me out, yeah? 'Cause if you want my power, that means you want me to make like a suit of armor and protect my owner, right? Dumbest thing I've ever heard, ya dig? I may be armor, but it hurts to get hit, and it scratches my awesome gleaming body! What kind of owner are we talking about anyway? Is it someone, like, worthy of me?>

Chris's smile froze on her face. "...I, uh, can't tell you for sure, but probably it's someone full of righteousness and courage and kindness—"

<Not what I meant! I don't give a crap about what's inside! It's looks that matter! Are we talking big boobs? Hourglass figure? Just so you know, underage kids get a big *N-O* from me. Y'know, maybe I'm more into the cute girls than the really hot ones. My last owner was a fighter, and I think I'd like to do that again. Minimal clothes on under the armor, please.>

......

"Hey, do we really need such lowbrow armor? Let's just leave him at the bottom of the sea."

"It's not that I don't sympathize, Lowly Assistant, but this is a Sacred Treasure here. In fact, I definitely *do* sympathize, but just grin and bear it."

Apparently, we were destined to take this ridiculous suit of armor home.

Without another word, I started pulling the Bubble Wrap out of my bag...

<Hmm? Hey now, what's the dark-haired kid up to? ...Y'know, do you think you could tell me exactly who you guys are? Come to think of it, didn't you say something about breaking in here in the middle of the night?>

Aigis seemed to be talking in my direction.

"You got it. We're burglars, and we're here to bust you out of this room and give you to a proper master. You're sacred armor, a Sacred Treasure, right? Then do your damn job."

Chris watched me pulling out the Bubble Wrap from the corner of her eye as she worked on Aigis's chains.

"Not too many girls get sent here from Japan, so I'm not certain we're going to be able to accommodate everything you're asking for," she said. "But if any young women do come through, we'll be sure to prioritize you…"

It was at that moment that Aigis exclaimed, in a voice loud enough to be heard around the entire house:

\<I'm bein' kidnapped!!\>

I thought about pointing out that you don't *kidnap* a suit of armor, but I gave it up.

Chapter 3

May Everything Be Left to This Capable Adviser!

1

Last night was awful.

Aigis's shouting brought the entire household running, and Chris and I had to flee without the chance to steal anything at all.

I was pretty sure nobody saw us, but I'm never entirely comfortable being on a wanted list.

I got back home before dawn, and when the excitement of the episode had finally worn off, I lay down to...

"Good morning! Hey, Kazuma, wake up—it's morning!"

...*try* to sleep, only to be rudely interrupted.

Aqua's announcement came just as I was burying myself under the covers, so I flung open the door and lit into her.

"Do you know how early it is?! I haven't slept a wink all night, and I'm finally going to get some rest, so pipe down!"

She normally slept almost as late as I did, but I had a suspicion as to why she was up so early on this particular day.

"Oh, you haven't slept, Kazuma? I guess that makes sense. After all, I already know why."

I was stunned to hear her say that. I was sure no one had seen me come back to the mansion—could she have noticed me?

For that matter, how did she know I had been out thieving?

Maybe she wasn't the complete idiot I took her for.

"You were too excited to sleep because you knew preparations for the festival were starting today! Don't worry. It's nothing to be embarrassed about—it's a festival, after all!"

I guess I was the idiot for thinking I had to be wary of her.

Aqua, full of excitement, pulled the curtains open with a *whoosh* and tossed me some clothes to change into despite my unwillingness to do so.

"Can't the festival preparations wait until afternoon? Why do they have to start so early…?"

"Kazuma, what are you talking about? We're adventurers, aren't we? We're preparing for monster hunting, obviously!"

…?

"Weren't we talking about preparations for your festival?"

"That's exactly what we're talking about."

I had no idea what we were talking about anymore.

"Darkness and Megumin are ready already! Come on, Kazuma—get it together! Otherwise we're all going to be late!"

Be late?

Seriously, what was going on here?

I changed my clothes, as instructed…

We arrived at the Adventurers Guild, and I opened the door to discover it was packed inside.

"…Look at this. Why would there be so many people here today?"

The place was overflowing with adventurers looking at the bulletin board for work.

This made zero sense.

It hadn't been that long since we had all gone and hunted the Kowloon Hydra together. Their purses should have been stuffed.

And yet…

"Those going to hunt the Lesser Wyvern nesting in the mountains, over here, please! We especially need a Thief who can use Bind and, given that this is a flying enemy, an Archer who knows Deadeye! The reward is commensurate with the enemy's strength! We have six more spaces available!"

"Bug-type monsters are swarming the forest! There are a lot of them, so we need plenty of people! This is going to be a large-scale hunt involving about a dozen people—any class, any level!"

"There are also a lot of herbivorous monsters on the plain—I do hope some of you will help take care of them. If left to their own devices, they'll attract the huge monsters that prey on them; we need to get rid of them before that happens. The Guild is currently offering a variety of free items to support this effort! The hunt reward is also greater than normal! This is your chance to make some easy money!"

"Hey, what's going on here?" I asked.

Aqua replied, "Obviously, the festival can't be held safely if we don't get rid of the monsters around here, so everyone's in a frenzy. Strong monsters appear in the winter, but in the summer, it's weak monsters that are the most active. This season even sees an increase in hunt rewards—it's a great opportunity for adventurers to save up a little money."

Huh, okay.

But that still didn't really explain why everyone was here instead of lounging around after the windfall from the hydra.

…Ah. I saw a group of adventurers I recognized and went over to them.

"What's up, guys—you're here, too? I know Dust doesn't have any money, but why are the rest of you with him? You should be rolling in cash."

It was the party of Dust and his companions.

Keith, checking to make sure his bow was in good working order, looked at me, a little puzzled. "I would have expected you to be first in line for a hunt this big, Kazuma."

…Why me?

"Yeah, it's kind of weird that you're not more excited about this, Kazuma (Mr. Regular-at-*That*-Shop). This time of year, most male adventurers forget everything else and go on these huge hunts." This from Dust, who was sharpening his sword with an uncommonly serious expression.

"What's the big deal? Are you guys that excited about the festival?"

"Festival? Ah, the female adventurers are busy clearing out the monsters around here so the festival can be held. A lot of the ladies are faithful Eris followers, you know. But for us men, it's not like that. All the guys here want to go into the forest to hunt monsters."

The forest? Wouldn't around town be a much better place to hunt monsters than in the woods...?

Come to think of it, with all the other adventurers working so hard, maybe we could just take it easy.

I was thinking it was getting about time to go home.

There was one male staff member handing out support items to everyone in the crowded Guild who said, "Everyone, hunting the monsters that are currently swarming the woods is an especially serious responsibility, so please do your best! Whether or not we can enjoy a nice, peaceful festival this year is in your hands! Please help with our monster overpopulation problem...!"

Apparently, this was his way of encouraging the adventurers.

"...Say," I said, "how are killing these monsters and having a pleasant summer related?"

Aqua looked at me, puzzled. "Hmm? Because if there are too many monsters around, people won't be able to work in the nearby woods, right?"

"Yeah, I get that, but that would be more than just a problem for the woods, right?"

Megumin had a response to that. "Cicadas."

Just one word, spoken with fear and loathing.

Cicadas.

So the singing, insectoid heralds of summer existed in this world, too.

"Yes," Darkness interjected, suddenly looking very serious. "If there are too many monsters in the woods, the cicada catchers can't do their jobs. If the cicada catchers can't do their jobs, then obviously the cicadas fly over to town. And the cicada migration usually happens to coincide with festival season."

"Okay, but who cares about cicadas? Aren't they a quintessential part of summer? They live in the ground for ages, then in summer they pop up and make their raucous-yet-short-lived music. Don't torment them just because they're a little annoying. That's human ego at work, and I hate that kind of thinking… In order to do my part in leaving those bugs alone, I'm going to go home and go to sleep."

As I spoke, I grabbed Darkness and Megumin both by the collar in order to drag them with me.

"Oh yeah," Aqua said, crossing her arms. "I forgot that you're a stupid jerk who doesn't know the first thing about this world, Kazuma. Well, listen to me. The cicadas here are on steroids. Japanese cicadas live for about a week. But the ones here, hopped up on magical energy and vitality, can live for up to a month."

Okay, so they liked to live large.

"So what? I'm sure there's some kind of catch, right?" I said. "Like maybe the droppings they leave behind when they start flying smell really bad or something. But hey, even bugs have to answer nature's call. And so what if they live for a month? Leave the poor things alone."

Megumin and Darkness looked at each other. They seemed to wonder if I was being serious.

"Excuse me, Kazuma," Aqua said. "There are two major differences between the cicadas here and the ones in Japan. For starters, the cicadas here are much louder. I'd say several times as loud as the ones you know."

So they're louder. Big deal.

…Wait, actually, I can see how that would be kind of annoying…

"And also…the cicadas here chirp all night as well as all day."

That sounds super-annoying!

2

We were in the woods near town.

A Guild staff member was directing a great many adventurers from the center of the forest.

"All right, frontliners with confidence in their Defense, cover your bodies in monster-attractant potions, please. Kindly bear in mind that although we're dealing with insect-type monsters, there are a lot of them, so don't let down your guard!"

Apparently, a quest like this was called a Large-Scale Hunt. When a group of monsters had grown too numerous for a single adventuring party to deal with, several parties would come together under the direction of a Guild staff member to get rid of them.

Normally, staff didn't go out in the field, but it seemed they could and would when a leader was needed in cases like this. To be fair, many adventurers were people who liked to do things their own way and didn't have a lot of patience for cooperation; without Guild staff to lead them, an effort like this could quickly descend into bickering.

As was happening now, for example.

"I, as acting governor, shall draw off all the monsters! Yes, this is my very duty as protector of the people! So give me all your potions!"

"No way—these aren't just for attracting monsters. If you use too much, you'll get attacked by everything under the sun."

"Th-that would be exactly what I desire!"

As *would* happen when you had someone like this involved.

"Hey, perv, don't get in the way of Guild business," I said. "You only need to protect our party."

"Ohhh! But summer monsters are so cute! I'm begging you, Kazuma, for pity's sake…!"

I grabbed Darkness before she could make any more demands and dragged her away.

Including my party and me, there were about thirty of us gathered there. It looked like most of the parties were made up of four or five people. The toughest-looking members of each group were dousing themselves with potions.

Darkness followed them, taking the potions she'd been given, and…

"…H-hey, you… Were you listening to the Guild person?"

Darkness was taking the potions, of which she seemed to have received more than her fair share, and applying them liberally to herself.

Despite my annoyed tone, Darkness replied, "Heh-heh. I can't spend every day telling you to work and then fail to stand in the vanguard myself. Crusaders are living shields. I'll take on every attack. But hey, it looks like you're actually kind of into this today. I'll keep you safe, so go slaughter the enemy with complete peace of mind!"

Darkness actually sounded kind of cool. Maybe she was really excited to finally be on a quest again. She gave a fearless smile, full of confidence.

"Well, obviously," I said. "When it comes to the safety of the townspeople, I'm sorry, but those monster cicadas are just going to have to die. I think you'll find I'm a little bit different today—just watch and see!"

Darkness was right: Somewhere along the line, I had gotten pretty fired up about this.

When I had learned how the cicadas of this world behaved, I understood why all the other guys were so eager to do this.

They were cicadas.

That's right: If they cried and chirped all night, then of course a certain establishment specializing in sweet dreams would be unable to provide their services.

And apparently, this would go on for an entire month.

Darkness and I seemed to have set the tone.

"The both of you are full of vim and vigor, I see. In that case, I shall show you that I will vanquish more monsters than anyone. Kazuma, just you watch!"

Megumin gave an equally confident smile, as if she thought she was competing with us.

I knew how this sort of thing went. Obviously, next would be…

"...? What? Why's everyone looking at me?"

"Huh? ...Oh, no reason. I was just thinking that this is right about when you usually get carried away and do something stupid."

Aqua, who was acting surprisingly mature, replied, "Excuse me, but just what do you take me for? I *am* capable of learning, you know. Wait and see. You three are getting carried away, and by the end of this hunt, it's going to cost you... Whereas I, ever intelligent, have learned. I've learned that getting carried away never leads to anything good."

"?!"

I could hardly believe my own ears. Was *Aqua*—the same Aqua who could get us in trouble no matter what we were doing, who could attract the undead just by standing around—was she...?!

To see Aqua grow up like this caused the tears to well in my eyes...

"?! Wh-what's wrong?! What on earth is going on?! Hey, Kazuma, why are you crying?"

I averted my eyes from Aqua's anxious jabbering, rubbing them gently, full of appreciation for my companion's genuine growth.

Maybe Darkness and Megumin couldn't hear what Aqua and I were saying, because they were looking at us in confusion.

"All adventurers! The first wave of monsters has arrived! We have plenty of insecticide ready. Let the hunt begin!" the Guild staff member's voice rang out.

Insect-like monsters were approaching us, loosing earsplitting cries as they moved to attack the people who had enemy-attractant potions slathered all over them.

"Ugh! Wait...! There's so many of them! Backup, somebody!" an adventurer shouted.

I looked to see them being attacked by a flying beetle the size of a small dog. And that was plenty big enough to be terrifying.

I'd heard that the horns of a flying beetle could punch through the windshield of a moving car. I didn't know what made the beetles around here so much bigger, but they seemed likely to be proportionately more troublesome.

As I watched in contemplation, the flying bugs plowed on. They twisted their little bodies as if they were going to start spinning, their horns thrusting upward...!

"Hrgh?!"

One adventurer took a horn to the stomach and started writhing in pain.

There was a screech of metal; the adventurer had been wearing armor. But even so...

"Eeeyowch! Dammit, he stabbed me in the stomach, even if it was only a little bit! Watch out—they'll punch right through cheap plate mail!"

As the adventurer fought back tears, I saw the bug lodged firmly in his armor.

These beetles really knew how to hit where it hurt!

Other adventurers quickly teamed up to extract the beetle from the first guy's armor. At the same time, the wounded man began to glow faintly.

"Huh...?! ...Ooh, healing magic!" The adventurer was surprised to discover his pain disappearing; maybe Aqua had healed him.

Next, the bodies of all the adventurers acting as our shields began to glow as well. Aqua was casting support magic on all of them.

What's with Aqua today? She's actually being useful...!

I was seized by a mixture of surprise and admiration.

"I can handle twenty of them! Twenty, I say!! Bring me more, more!"

Smack in the middle of those acting as our shields was my very own Crusader, stopping more attacks than any of them and shouting happily while she did it.

Today, Darkness seemed reliable and even a little bit cool, just like she'd said she would be.

My companions were showing sides of themselves I'd never expected. Far be it from me to be the only one who didn't get in on the action.

I took the insecticide I'd been given by the Guild, which came in a device made of bamboo and shaped a bit like a water pistol.

Then I squirted it at the oncoming bugs.

Adventurers around me did the same thing, trying to support our protectors.

It wasn't just horned beetles flying at us. There were creatures that looked like stag beetles and others that looked like praying mantises. There was a variety of others as well, all of them much, much bigger than normal. You might think they were just bugs, but at that size, they definitely qualified as monsters.

As the casualties piled up, Aqua did her best to keep healing. She wasn't even getting all carried away; she was quiet and businesslike. I brought my insecticide to bear, hoping to back her up, when I felt a tug on my sleeve.

"Is it not time yet? Kazuma, has my moment not yet come?!"

Megumin, seeing everyone else hard at work, was getting impatient to let off her explosion. I was sure she was eager to show what she could do. But…

"I'm sorry, but I don't think you'll have a moment today. We're in the middle of a forest, remember? If you use your magic, you'll take out half the trees in the area. So just be quiet and—"

"*Explosion*!!!"

Megumin intoned her magic spell as if she had never had any intention of letting me finish.

From high above our heads came a massive roar and a blinding flash of light.

A violent wash of air came down along with them, leaving behind it a bunch of toppled adventurers and Darkness.

Apparently, the small bug-type monsters couldn't withstand the force of the shock, because they had all dropped to the ground and stopped moving.

There was a lot of moaning going on. Aqua had managed to recover and was hurrying busily from one person to the next, casting healing magic.

Megumin, from her place collapsed on the ground beside me, had only this to say:

"Megumin has leveled up."

"You dumbass!" I sat up, angry, and dragged the all-too-pleased Megumin up with me. "Why the hell would you do it when I said not to?! Just look at this mess! You need to apologize to everyone right now!"

"It's because you told me I would never have a chance here, Kazuma. The adventurers of this town are already accustomed to my explosions, so they're fine."

Megumin was boldly defiant, and what was worse, she was right: The adventurers scattered on the ground were pulling themselves to their feet without so much as a word of complaint.

This is some group…

As I approached them, Darkness was trying to get up off the ground, but her heavy armor was giving her a rough time.

As she lay there struggling, she said, "…What's this? My body is tingling." She looked puzzled…

I glanced at her armor, and my eyes just about bugged out of my head. "Holy crap…! Your armor! You've got ants all over your armor!"

Darkness's landing spot on the ground was swarming with ants. This was probably what came of ignoring the staff and slathering herself with every enemy-attractant potion she could find.

I took a step back, but Darkness tried to catch the eyes of Aqua and me. "Ahh…! Wai— Kazuma, help me! It—it tickles! The ants must be getting into my armor; hurry and spray me with insecticide, or Create Water, or…!"

With her armor on, she couldn't scratch herself, but neither could she quickly take her armor off—so she was reduced to thrashing and yelling.

It sounded like a pain to deal with, and besides, she'd brought this on herself. I ignored her.

The Guild staff member, who had also been knocked over by the explosion, stood up without a word, perhaps accustomed to us rowdy adventurers pulling stunts like this. "Good work, everyone; now get ready for the second wave..."

...*Second wave?*

The Guild person sounded casual, but along with the announcement, we could hear a distinct humming of insect wings. The shaking and quaking from the explosion had presumably upset the rest of the bugs in the forest.

"...Well, this is no good."

"Waaaaah, Kazumaaa! I have a really, really bad feeling about this!" Aqua, belying how calm she had been all day, cried to me with an expression of distinct unease.

She wasn't wrong, though: We soon saw hundreds of bugs, who were all very angry that we were invading their territory...!

"Fall back!" I shouted. "Fall baaack!" The adventurers and Guild staff around me scattered in all directions.

"—Ohhh... *Sniff*... And I tried so hard this time... I was a good girl and didn't get carried away or anything, and still..."

The lot of us was on the road home.

I heaved a sigh, dragging along Aqua, whose hair was in disarray from the swarm of insects. Riding on my back was Megumin, who was still in awfully high spirits over having taken out an entire army of monsters all by herself.

Although they had ultimately ended up in some danger, the rest of the adventurers had been part of a major hunt in relative safety. The massive reward for slaying all those monsters would be split equally among everyone, so they were all looking pretty happy, too.

And then there was...

"Mn… Unf…! *Pant… Pant…* Kazuma… K-Kazuma, this is an entirely new sensation… This is completely new to me…"

Maybe there were still ants in Darkness's armor, because she was bright red and running her stupid mouth—and despite her complaints that it hurt-tickled until just a little while ago, she seemed altogether pleased with the situation at the moment.

Remind me again why I gave up everything I owned to rescue this pervert.

3

The days after the hunt were both busy and fulfilling. Mornings, we would go out hunting monsters, and in the afternoons, we would busy ourselves with preparations for the festival.

I wasn't normally big on monster hunting, but for the sake of my beloved shop… Er, I mean, for the sake of the upcoming festival, it hardly seemed much to ask.

Maybe even a *hikikomori* like me wanted to experience the fun of a school culture festival?

I met with the other leaders of the downtown district on a near-daily basis, giving them a wealth of advice, all purely from the innocent desire for this celebration to succeed.

One Week Until the Festival

"—As your adviser, I think it would be an excellent way to increase sales if all your salesgirls were wearing swimsuits!" I slammed the table with my fist, my adviser passion burning.

"I think that's a fine idea, a fine idea indeed, but! If we overdo it, won't the police have something to say about it?!"

"How can you have a festival if you're afraid of mere words?! As our esteemed adviser says, it would certainly increase sales! And what self-respecting merchant knows of a way to increase sales but doesn't take advantage of it?!"

"I'm sorry, but I think the president's concern is warranted. It would be problematic if the desire for short-term profit caused next year's festival to be curtailed in any way... Damn! If only there was some excuse to get those girls in swimsuits..."

The president was worried.

The other council members were arguing.

And as I watched them, a plan came together in my mind.

"I've got an idea."

That changed the tone *real* quick.

"You do?!"

"What is it, dear adviser?!"

I looked back at them. "The celebration this year is partly the Aqua Appreciation Festival. That's right: The name of the goddess of water is on the marquee."

Everyone drew a collective breath.

"So we have salesgirls in swimsuits here and there, and we splash them with water. Then we explain that we had them wear swimsuits because you can get them wet. Besides, I hear the festival is held at the hottest time of year. Well, we wouldn't want anyone to get heatstroke, would we? If anyone tries to object, we just say, 'So when they collapse from overheating, you'll take responsibility?' Bureaucrats hate the word *responsibility*—that'll quiet them down."

"Brilliant! Mr. Adviser, you're a genius!"

"When this festival is over, I want you to come be an adviser for my establishment!"

The council chamber was filled with the sound of applause.

"—Hey, Kazuma," Darkness said. "The festival committee sent us something that says 'Guidelines for Heatstroke Prevention and Outline of the Aqua Appreciation Festival.' You're a member of that committee, right? What's going on here?"

"Oh yeah, it's supposed to be real hot during the festival. They're going to be spraying water here and there to keep people cool, and you can't expect the salesgirls to wear their usual work clothes in that situation. What if the water made their underwear transparent? Swimsuits will keep anyone from being embarrassed. I never got a chance to be part of a festival like this in my own country. So it's really important to me that this one succeeds..."

"O-oh, I see. Sorry, my gut instinct thought something weird was going on. But if that's the case, then I understand, and I give my permission. You're right—this is the first summer festival we all get to experience together. Of course we want it to succeed."

And thus I managed to get Darkness, still not quite accustomed to being governor, on board.

Three Days Until the Festival

Not everything went so smoothly for me as adviser. I had some pretty serious arguments with the operations committee as well.

"All of our explosion-magic users have been sent to reinforce the vicinity of the capital against recent activity by the Demon King's army," the president of the committee was saying. "We simply don't have the firepower for fireworks this year. We'll have to cancel them."

That provoked a vicious response from me.

"Idiot! How can you even think of canceling the fireworks?! Fireworks mean *YUKATA*, get it?! And a festival isn't a festival without *YUKATA*!!"

"Please, Sir Adviser, calm down! When you say *yukata*, do you mean *those yukata*? The famous light summer robes from a far country?"

"It's just fireworks and *YUKATA*. Is such a big deal?"

"I understand that you're looking forward to these robes of yours. And I've heard that it is customary to wear *yukata* while watching fireworks displays. But without any users of Explosion available, I don't think there's anything we can do. I don't even know if there are any users of blasting magic around here…"

"Just lobbing a Fireball up in the air won't amount to much…"

I looked around at them, and that was when I hit on a plan.

"I've got an idea. One of my party members knows explosion magic."

"No, absolutely not! That blast would obliterate the entire festival!"

"I take it back—you're no genius! You're a fool!"

"We should never have asked a man like this to be our adviser. What was I thinking…?"

The committee set about ridiculing my plan.

I grabbed the president by the collar of his shirt. "Just say that again, you jackass—you're the one who oughta quit! A fireworks display is central to every man's romantic fantasies! It's an absolutely crucial part of any summer! Watching fireworks with a girl in a *yukata*! It's just the moment where you can casually take her hand and she won't even mind—and you want to skip it?! What the hell are you thinking?!"

"Then come up with another plan, you little shit. A useful one! Hey, you'd better lower that arm—does an adventurer dare to commit violence against a civilian?"

"Let's get him! He may be rich, but he's not strong! Don't let him get away!"

Like I said, we didn't always see eye to eye.

"'Application for Permission to Use Explosion Potion'…? Hey, Kazuma, what do you plan to use something like that for? Isn't that dangerous? Hey, wait a second… Why are you covered in bruises?"

"We need the potion for the festival. Everyone's hopes are riding on me; I can't let this celebration fail."

"R-right. You look so serious; you must mean it. I'll grant permission. But…seriously, why are you so badly injured?"

"There are some things a man just has to fight for. These wounds are marks of pride for me. I got them defending what matters most."

"Um, okay, then. I won't ask for the details. Something tells me it's better that I don't."

Persuading Darkness to go along with what I wanted was just one of the many tasks that filled my days.

I realized, on reflection, that I had never really gotten to experience a culture festival in middle school. Maybe it was selfish of me, but this was a way of getting back just a little bit of the student life I had never gotten to enjoy. To be perfectly honest, the payment I was receiving as adviser was secondary.

I turned away from Darkness, who still looked a bit concerned, and headed for my room. Along the way, I offered up a prayer that this festival would go smoothly.

…Until the Festival

At long last, the festival would be held the next day, and this was the final day on which the committee would meet. During this brief time in which I would culminate my role as adviser, I brought a plan to the companions with whom I had argued and fought so much.

"Where I come from, there was a place called Asakusa that used to hold a Samba Carnival. Girls in provocative costumes would dance wildly while parading down the street…"

"Don't lie to us! Whoever heard of such a festival?! You're just saying whatever you want! What kind of adviser are you? You're just some horny kid!"

"The other day, he claimed that there's a festival where women carry around a giant sculpture of the male member—preposterous! A festival like that would be madness!!"

The other members of the committee were getting restless, but I pounded the table as I made my rebuttal. "It's true, every word! Don't go around calling people liars when they aren't! And come on, the Eris Festival is just too plain! You're really telling me the whole thing consists of everybody going to the Eris Church to pray? There's got to be something else, something eye-catching—portable shrines slamming into one another or something!"

"Festivals are sacred occasions, not the insanity you're imagining!"

"Making money is certainly important, but I think we're at risk of losing something even more valuable!"

"The ideas you come up with are too over-the-top! I'm not saying there can't be a little bawdiness, but can't you be subtler?!"

That night...

I was having my now-customary discussion with Darkness...

"Hey, Kazuma, do you have a moment?" she said.

"I guess. What's up?"

"I don't understand what this proposed 'costume parade' is."

I had been expecting as much.

"They say the goddess Eris comes down to our world in an assumed form and does things for the benefit of the people here without anybody knowing. You've heard that story, right?"

"Yeah, sure... It's a famous fairy tale among Eris followers. That's why every year at this time, the town is full of people dressed like Lady Eris, so she can incarnate herself in her true form to come enjoy the festival. No one will know it's her among all the costumes."

Huh, and here I thought everyone was just into cosplay. I didn't know there was a story like that behind it.

"Well, the costume parade is based on that custom, but it'll help spice up the festival a little bit. The costumes don't have to look like Lady Eris. They could look like a hero, or a queen, or the goddess Aqua, or anything at all. In my country, we had a festival called Comiket, and you'd see all sorts of cosplay there."

"I—I see. I guess the part about wanting to make things more exciting makes sense to me. But still…this festival *is* about honoring a goddess, and I'm a little concerned about this application for permission to dress up as a succubus…"

"What are you talking about? Remember, this is a big festival. Goddesses aren't the only ones who want to get out and about sometimes. It's a festival, so why worry? If you have a few girls in sexy costumes wandering around town, just chalk it up to having a good time."

"A good time… Hmm? Wait, hang on. What are you talking about? It almost sounds like you want beings other than the goddess to be able to join in…"

"Don't think about it—just sign the stinking paper. This is a special request from the male adventurers of this town! Plus, if we can get this idea approved, I know some lovely ladies who promised to do *real* succubus cosplay!"

"Who exactly are these lovely ladies? And why are you so intent on this?! Fine, fine, I understand! I just don't know what kind of girls would dress up like *that*…"

And so, as frantic as it was, preparations for the festival proceeded as planned.

Until finally, the day arrived…

4

"All right, Axel, I know you've been waiting for this! Are you ready? It's time for the Eris and Aqua Appreciation Festival!"

"Whoooooooooo!"

The MC's voice echoed from a magical amplifying device. At the same moment, magical spells were thrown into the sky to celebrate, and they were matched on the ground by cheering and shouting.

"Is it morning already…?"

It was the day of the start of the festival.

In an attempt to make up for the time spent working all day every day, since the night before I had been binging the game Aqua brought back from Crimson Magic Village. The ruckus outside alerted me that morning had come.

I came downstairs, famished, to find Megumin eating breakfast by herself.

"Good morning, Kazuma. Aqua and Darkness and now you— everyone's up very early this morning."

"I'm not exactly *up*; I've just been playing a game in my bed since last night. Are you telling me Aqua and Darkness are awake already? I don't see them anywhere. Did they go out?"

"Aqua was too excited to sleep all night, so she went out as soon as it was light."

Like a kid who couldn't wait to go on a field trip.

"When I told Darkness that Aqua had left, she dashed out in a hurry. I think she was going to make sure the Axis Church didn't pull any weird stunts."

"Life's been rough for her since she became acting governor, huh? Are you going to go see the festival, Megumin?"

"No. I am thinking of going to see Yunyun, who likely has no one to take her to the festival and is presumably on the verge of tears by now. I will wander back and forth nearby, not specifically offering to go to the festival, teasing her with her inability to just come out and invite me. Would you like to join me, Kazuma?"

"Geez, if you're gonna go that far, then just go with her. I'm gonna take an all-day nap, then check out the shops in the evening."

"What you're describing does not sound like a nap, but… By the way, Kazuma, are you available on the third night of the festival?" Megumin had finished her breakfast and was calmly sipping some tea.

"The third night? I'll probably be checking out the shops again. Why?"

"Oh, it's just that there's a fireworks display on the third night. I can't imagine a fireworks display involving the Axis Church could possibly occur without incident, so we won't be sure until the day of… But if it is safe, would you like to go see it with me?"

Before I could answer, Megumin disappeared into the kitchen with her breakfast utensils.

…Hey, there is *going to be a fireworks display, isn't there?*
Going to see a festival fireworks display with a girl.
Whoa, it's almost like normal adolescence!

That night…

Unable to sleep because of the unexpected "fireworks event," I found myself uncharacteristically intimidated by the bustle of town.

Crowded public spaces were the natural enemy of the *hikikomori*.

And the closer I got to the merchant district, the more crowded it became.

At the entrance to the Axel merchant district, a huge curtain had been hung, inscribed with the words ERIS APPRECIATION FESTIVAL in towering letters.

The words AQUA APPRECIATION FESTIVAL had been added beside them in much smaller letters.

Thinking I should start by seeing how things were going, I headed for the area set off for the Axis Church.

It was full twilight, and the town was ablaze with lights. The streets of the business district were even livelier than usual, full of adventurers and townspeople and vendors and every type of person. There were shop stalls everywhere you looked and a whole lot of noise.

I hoped Aqua's area would be just as exciting.

Unfortunately, over by where Aqua and her friends had their shop, it looked like some kind of disagreement had broken out.

5

"I'm afraid you simply cannot sell something like this without permission! Why must you Axis disciples always be nothing but trouble?"

"'Something like this'? How rude! Our Lady Aqua was so kind as to come up with the idea for this shop, and you come here and badmouth it?!"

Cecily was the one involved in the fight. She was in the middle of an argument with one of the policemen patrolling the festival.

"Hey, you, what are you doing?" I said. "I told you to make things exciting, not get in a big fight. Why is it you people can never be satisfied if you're not getting yourselves in trouble with the police every time I look away?"

Cecily looked like she was about to be arrested. When she saw me, she exclaimed, "Oh, perfect timing! Listen to me, good Kazuma, this man is giving me trouble—he wants me to shut down this shop!"

"What do you mean, 'trouble'? There's no way I can permit this!"

What in the world could they be fighting about?

I glanced at the shop in question to discover a washbasin full of water, with tadpoles swimming in it.

"...What's this?"

The animals looked awfully large for tadpoles.

In that moment...

"Lady Aqua told us. She said goldfish scooping was essential at festivals. We didn't understand exactly what goldfish scooping was, but I've tried to re-create it as best I can. I couldn't find any wild goldfish, so I settled for tadpoles and opened this shop..." As Cecily spoke, she looked at me as if begging me to do something.

What was the point in fishing for tadpoles? In fact, wait a second, weren't these...?

"Hey, aren't these a little big for tadpoles? Are they really just tadpoles?"

As if in response, the officer said, "Come on, you can't sell young Giant Toads here! They'll grow up before you know it! If you sell these small ones, in a few months the town will be overrun with frogs!"

"Let's put some insecticide in this pool," I suggested, following my first instinct, but Cecily tried desperately to stop me.

"Please don't destroy my shop! Lady Aqua was sure you would be happy to experience such a nostalgic pastime! Don't you love goldfish scooping?!"

"Yeah, emphasis on *goldfish*. Who would want to catch these ugly things? If we put them back in the wild, they'll grow up and cause all kinds of problems, so if you don't want me to just kill them, then get rid of them somewhere far, far away from here! Didn't you guys insist that if I got you permission for this festival, everything else would be fine?"

Cecily snickered at that. "Surely you don't think this is the only shop the Axis Church has here? For the sake of this day, we enlisted Axis followers from all over town to put their heads together!"

Cecily began pointing, highlighting more than thirty shops of all different types. Startled to realize there were more Axis followers than just Cecily in this town, I thought of certain other species where the presence of one was likely to indicate thirty more.

Surprisingly, though, there were a lot of visitors at each of the stalls, and it looked genuinely lively. There was an instant where I almost admired them and what must have been a great deal of hard work—until I noticed there was something odd about those shops…

"Who wants to try grilled kraken?" one woman shouted. "Young krakens grilled up just for you, a most unusual treat! Try one; they're delicious!"

"Hey, isn't this just normal grilled squid? It doesn't taste any different…"

"What are you talking about—have you ever tried real kraken? This is what it tastes like, I assure you. You have the guarantee of the Axis Church!"

"Come one, come all, and see what's in my stall! Behold the crea-ture caught by one very brave Axis disciple: a bizarre half-breed, the offspring of a fishy merman and the half-human, half-fish mermaid! …Oh! Honored customer, you mustn't turn violent inside the shop!"

"Like hell. Gimme my money back! It's just a big fish in a tank!"

"I told you: It's the offspring of a merman and a mermaid!"

…Well, that went south in a hurry.

"Do your sharpshooting here! Hit the target right between the eyes and win a—"

"Hey, the character you're using for a target looks just like Lady Eris! Does your blasphemy against her know no bounds?!"

"Huh, Eris followers trying to antagonize us on the very first day of the festival! Patrolmaaan, come over here, please! I need you to arrest this Eris follow— Hey, what're you doing? You're supposed to get rid of this woman, not my shop…!"

………So you had one guy already getting shut down by the police. And then there was—

"Hey, lady, is this a real dragon?"

"Yes, of course it is. There's a craze for dragon raising in the Axis Church right now, you know. Only five hundred eris each. You should buy one."

And then there was the moron who had painted some lizards she'd caught nearby and was trying to convince passing kids they were dragons.

"Huh? Five hundred eris? That's my entire allowance. I won't be able to buy anything else, so forget it. Plus, they look an awful lot like lizards."

"That's your choice, I guess. But then these poor little things will be leftovers. And you can hardly just release an unsold dragon into the wild; it would be much too dangerous. They'll have to go to a shelter somewhere… And if they still can't find owners, I'm sure they'll have to be put down, the poor dragons…"

Cowed by this ridiculous charade, the kid started to sweat.

"N-no way! Those are just lizards, aren't they?! You can set them loose anywhere!" He looked like he was about to cry, but the idiot running the shop decided to appeal to the goodness in a child's heart.

"Heavens no, these are genuine dragons! Are you sure you won't buy one? Can you live with yourself, not doing that for them?"

"Ergh… B-but if I buy one, I won't have any allowance left…"

"So you won't buy one, is that it?! Believe me—you'll regret it! Oh, you poor dragons, now you'll go to a shelter for sure!"

"I'll send that dumb *chick* of yours to a shelter! Grah! What do you think you're doing to these kids, you jerk?!"

I smacked Aqua on the head.

6

"You were the victim of a fake dragon–selling scheme, and then you turn around and try to victimize others the same way?"

"What are you talking about, Kazuma? Don't you know? A little bit of ripping off and swindling is par for the course at a festival. Doesn't that ever happen in Japan? And also, I'll have you know that Emperor Zel is a genuine dragon."

I put my head in my hands, our resident lizard vendor, Aqua, in tow.

I still hadn't found a single serious stall. I should have known it was a mistake to leave things to this group. Even with me diligently fanning the rivalry between the two churches, Aqua and her friends were simply too much of a risk.

"What you guys were up to doesn't even count as 'a little,' you idiot! Not only have you *not* made this festival more exciting, you've pissed off all our customers! And on top of that, Darkness said she was going to be looking around the festival personally. When that hardhead gets wind of this farce, you'd better believe the Axis Church will never be allowed to participate in a festival again."

That last detail seemed to finally alert Aqua to the gravity of the situation.

"W-well, how about this one, then? Come here, Kazuma—I've got faith in this shop! There's nothing shady about it, and it's making more money than anyone else!"

She dragged me over to a particular shop. It was a little stall in the far corner of the area that had been dedicated to the Axis Church.

To my surprise, there was an actual crowd around it.

…When I got a good look, though, my knees buckled.

There, her face drawn, was Chris.

"Chris was just wandering around, looking like she had plenty of free time, so I asked her to help out with this shop!"

What is she doing? I mean, seriously.

Why was the goddess of the Eris Church helping out at an Axis shop?

Chris was sitting there, hugging her knees, her expression dead. She waved to me weakly.

It looked like she was running some kind of lottery.

"Hey, another one! I want another one!"

"Wait your turn; I'm first! I've put a lot of money into this already!"

You bought a ticket, and if you got the lucky number, you could get back several times what you put in. It was a simple concept, but nonetheless, the shop had a lot of visitors, and for some reason, everyone was really getting into it.

One man held up several eris coins, then picked one of the three tickets Chris held out to him.

Tremblingly, he checked the number…

"Dammit, lost again! Hey, show me the other two!"

Chris did as he asked, revealing the numbers on the other two tickets. Both of them were winners.

Ah, so only one out of three lost. Most games like this involved a one-in-three chance of *winning*, but this shop actually gave customers the advantage.

But yet…

"All right, this time I'm going to win! I don't see anything fishy going on here, which means I have to get lucky eventually!"

"There's no sign that blessing magic's been cast anywhere, so why do we always lose…? Come on—let's quit this."

"Just one more time! I don't even have to make back what I put in; I'd be happy just to win once! I can't leave with nothing but misses!"

There was every indication the customers were at an advantage, yet they kept losing—and that both upset them and made it impossible for them to back out.

It was too bad for them, but they were facing...

"Okay, this is it! O Lady Eris, goddess of good fortune, please let me pick a winner this time! If I don't, I swear I'll convert to the Axis Church!"

"What?! W-wait just a second!" Chris exclaimed, but it was too late. The man was already grabbing a new ticket...!

"This is the one! ...Aaaarrrggghhh, dammit!! Screw stupid Lady Eriiis!"

"H-how could you?!"

I guess the guy lost again. He threw the ticket to the ground, shouting, while Chris sat there ready to cry.

"Excellent work, Chris—I knew it was worth forcing you to help me with this! Not only did you run the game, you even earned the Axis Church a new convert! You know, I got this really weirdly shaped rock from the Kowloon Hydra's cave, and I'd be willing to give it to you to thank you."

"I don't want it! Aww...my precious follower..."

I really couldn't fathom what she was doing here. Apparently, Aqua had come along with one of her selfish requests, and Chris hadn't been able to say no...

Then along came Cecily—the one who had previously been fighting with the police—completely ignoring the shocked Chris.

"Lady Aqua, what should we do...? Now that that one die-hard has given up, all the rest of the customers are following him... Perhaps it's time to resurrect my gelatinous-slime stall?"

"You're right... That might be our only choice."

"Hey, you two, quit trying to sell weird crap. I'll share a nice little piece of info with you!"

7

Bah, how did this happen?

I hadn't had any intention of doing any real work, but at this rate, the Axis people weren't going to be any match for the Eris followers. I'd wanted them to liven things up—but they were just going to ruin everything and get kicked out.

The Eris Church, on the other hand, seemed pretty pleased with itself, able to set up its stalls while spending no more than the price of materials.

There were choral groups singing songs of praise to Eris and people giving toasts and offering thanks to the goddess.

It didn't seem very, well, *new*. If anything, it felt like an old, established festival, and to look at the Eris followers, smiling and drinking wine in honor of their deity, it started to seem perfectly natural to have an Eris Appreciation Festival...

"—Come on, Kazuma. What am I supposed to do?"

"This is when you pull out those party tricks of yours—for once, your powers can come in handy. Once you've attracted enough customers, then come help with the cooking. Cecily can entertain the guests. Chris, maybe you could help us cook."

"Oh-ho, so I'll be drawing in customers," Aqua said. "You can trust me on that."

"I just need to rely on my looks and give those men the hard sell, is that it?" Cecily said. "Leave it to me."

"Oh, come on, do I still have to help?!"

After I had given instructions, I set about cooking. The smell of sauce drifted through the merchant quarter. People must have been drawn to it, because eventually...

"All right, next, please! Large green seaweed with plenty of mayonnaise! Hey, Aqua, chop some more cabbage for me! And, Chris, get on that pork!"

"Hey, Kazuma, why can't I work the pork?! This cabbage is too lively to handle!"

"I'm not exactly a cabbage expert myself! Come on, Lowly Assistant—I can do the grilling, so you handle the cabbage!"

Aqua was involved in a life-or-death struggle with the vegetables while, despite her complaining, Chris was chopping the pork skillfully.

"No choice, I guess," Aqua said. "Watch closely, Chris, and see how I wield this butcher's knife! …Mm, summer cabbage is so crispy. It's my favorite."

"*Munch…* Hmm, I think I like spring cabbage better. Winter cabbage is too violent for my tastes, and fall cabbage has too much of a tendency to fly away…"

"We're drowning in customers, and you guys are eating our supply?! Here you go. Thank you for waiting. One extra-large pork bits with noodles al dente!"

Once I started cooking, the stall grew more popular before my eyes.

The menu was that quintessential and beloved Japanese festival food: *yakisoba*, or fried noodles.

Thanks to the Japanese people who had come to this world, various earthly foods had made their way here, too. But although a lot of famous dishes like miso soup, fried chicken, and hamburgers were available, there were some that still hadn't been accounted for.

"This *yakisoba* is delicious!" one of the customers declared. "The sauce—mm!"

"I couldn't agree more—just smelling it makes me hungry!"

"Hey, man, hit me with an extra-large cabbage with al dente noodles and plenty of mayo!"

"Thank you very much; your order will be right up! Hey, Cecily, give me an order slip for that… Don't you eat the cabbage, too!"

Yakisoba sauce was apparently something new to the people of this world, and everyone seemed to be enjoying it. Maybe even the Japanese visitors who knew how to cook hadn't had any sauce recipes.

You didn't see a lot of specialty cuisine around here—things like

curry or *okonomiyaki* sauce, stuff where you had to mix a bunch of spices together.

So why was I able to make *yakisoba* sauce? Well...

"A food stall staffed by someone with the Cooking skill! This is one serious festival! Will the Axis Church be participating again next year, by any chance?"

"Isn't the chef Kazuma Satou? He's a pretty well-known adventurer. Guess he can cook, too."

That's right; I owed it to the skill I had picked up earlier.

I had taken the Cooking skill in hopes of raising my overall standard of daily living, but I had never expected it to come in handy at a time like this.

It wasn't a skill that most of the Japanese imports here took.

Or rather, it was one they *couldn't* take.

Because a bunch of OP cheaters would never deliberately stay as Adventurers, the weakest class.

The Eris Church seemed to value tradition in their festival, so I decided to go up against it with something more contemporary. The novelty, or maybe just the sheer unusualness of it, seemed remarkably well received, not to mention the fact that Cecily was casually wrapping the orders in application forms for the Axis Church.

Aqua's eyes sparkled as she took it all in.

"You hear that, Kazuma? They're praising Axis followers! This is all so fresh and new to me!"

"Who wants gelatinous slime on the side? Sweet, jiggly gelatinous slime!"

"Stoppit—that stuff's illegal! No weird toppings! Fa-ha-ha, how about that, Aqua? A human doing a little honest work is making all the money! No rip-offs needed—honesty is the best policy! ...Heck, with how popular this place is, maybe I should open a real restaurant! I know I already have so much money I never need to work again, but I just can't stop smiling!"

"Say, Lowly Assistant... It sort of seems like people are shifting away from the Eris booths and coming over here. I'm starting to question what I'm doing here…"

That night…

All of the Axis stalls got written up, with one exception: a modest *yakisoba* shop.

8

"—All right, so here are the sales for today."

""""Whaaaaaa—?!"""""

The staff of the downtown council had gathered in the council chamber. When the sales for the first day of the festival were reported, all of us, including me, let out a shout.

"That's nearly twice an average year—this festival is a huge success!"

"Our dear adviser was exactly right—getting the Axis and Eris Churches to go at it paid off big-time! Not that the Axis Church seems to have made a lot of money, but they sure provoked the Eris Church to take it up a notch."

"Gosh, it might have been nice if the Axis followers had worked a little harder, but this is still a strong result. There is one bright spot on the Axis side, though—this place calling itself Yakisobaya did really well. I hear it only just started this evening, but it's going to open earlier tomorrow. That means we can expect even better sales from it."

There might have been a lot of fighting in the run-up to the festival, but with results like this, everyone was all smiles as they looked at me. Apparently, because the merchants were handling this festival in lieu of the governor, a portion of any taxes raised during the festival would be paid out to them as a reward. And of course I, as adviser, was entitled to my share.

Frankly, to those of us on the committee, it didn't matter which of the churches "won" the festival, as long as we made money.

"About the fried-noodle place," I said. "Honestly, most of the Axis places were kind of worthless, so I re-created a dish from my country and sold that. You can count on me, as your adviser, for tomorrow, too. As a matter of fact, I have a special plan."

""""Oh-ho!"""""

The collective gaze turned to one of admiration.

"That's our Mr. Satou. I've heard you were connected to the recent success of Wiz's Magical Item Shoppe, and now I'm sure the rumor was true!"

"Ah, I can only tip my cap to such great success in such a short time!"

"I hope we can expect more of the same tomorrow!"

Heh, all this praise is kind of embarrassing me. I just wanted to re-create a Japanese-style festival.

"Well, just you watch. As your adviser, tomorrow, I'm going to get really serious."

""""Ooooh!"""""

And so the first day of the festival came to an end.

9

"…Hey, Kazuma. Are you perchance thinking of going to help the Axis Church?"

It was day two of the Eris and Aqua Appreciation Festival. It was still dark out, but people were already starting to gather in the downtown area.

As I prepared to leave the mansion, Darkness spoke to me in a leaden tone, with noticeable bags under her eyes.

"Yeah, that's the plan… What's with you? You look awful."

Darkness twisted around sleepily on the sofa. "I'm not surprised. I never dreamed being the governor would be so much work… This is suffering unlike anything I experienced before the festival. Did you know some moron released young Giant Toads into the lake that the Kowloon Hydra used to live in? I don't know what they were thinking… And then there were complaints of swindling at some freak show, and a haunted house where Axis followers dressed up as zombies and molested visitors…"

Crap. I recognized some of those problems.

"Then there were the reports of Axis disciples pushing over the shop stalls of Eris followers, demanding money from them to operate, a request for male staffers in swimsuits, and one place tricking kids into buying colored lizards…!"

I decided to make Darkness a cup of tea.

She took the cup and sipped at it listlessly, then let out a weak sigh.

"Thanks… I feel like I've aged a lot in the last few days…"

"That's rough… But just think: This is exactly how I feel every time I have to deal with the problems you guys cause. I mean, granted, I have a sneaking suspicion I was somehow involved with most of the trouble you had yesterday, but I think you'll find today is a lot easier. Hang in there a little longer."

Darkness must really have been feeling beat down, because her eyes started to brim at my show of comfort.

"Th-thank you so much…! At least you understand me…! On reflection, I see now how much trouble I've always caused you… Wait a second, what was that last thing you—?"

But I didn't have time to listen to the rest of whatever Darkness was saying; I had an Axis Church to energize.

When I arrived at the Axis Church area, I found a huge crowd but for totally different reasons than yesterday.

"Welcome, one and all! Get your *yakisoba* right here—festival food from a faraway land!"

"Wild octopus, caught in the forest and grilled for you! Thick-chopped and crunchy!"

"Shaved ice here! Delicious shaved ice!! We have strawberry, lemon, pineapple, red bean, and gelatinous-slime flavors!"

Okay, so there were some subtle differences, but what I saw before me looked almost exactly like a festival in Japan.

Aqua was quick to find me and rushed over clutching an ice bucket. "Oh, Kazuma, you're late! Just look at this crowd! The ice you made in the afternoon is all gone! I'll produce some water, so hurry up and freeze it!"

The various stalls looked just like what you would find in Japan—all right, maybe not *just* like them, but if they were a little weird in some ways, they were also definitely popular.

Excellent! I smell big sales today.

And that meant more money for me, the adviser.

"Looks like you're in high spirits today. If you acted like this all the time, you'd have way more followers. Isn't it nice to make people happy?" I grinned at Aqua as I used Freeze to produce ice.

Aqua, for her part, was smiling in a way I rarely saw from her. "Yes, and it's all thanks to you, Kazuma. Look how my dear Axis followers are smiling." She spoke with an earnestness I hadn't expected. "Kazuma, Kazuma! I'm so glad we were able to have this festival. Thank you for helping the Axis Church."

Then she gave me an innocent smile.

…Man. Did she go crazy from the excitement or something?

I thought about the cicada hunt, how she had learned that getting carried away only led to tears. There was something weird about Aqua recently.

Was it Emperor Zel?

Had having a child forced her to grow up?

Doubtful. She liked to go around calling that thing her kid, but all she had done was incubate an egg.

Still, as someone who stood to benefit financially from the success of this festival, I felt kind of conflicted to receive such sincere gratitude.

Changing the subject, I said, "S-say, you guys must be making out like bandits from all this popularity, huh? This would be a great opportunity to use the profits to build a cozy little Axis Church building, don't you think?"

"Honestly, we're not making all that much money. Remember what you said yesterday, Kazuma. 'A human doing a little honest work is making all the money! No rip-offs needed—honesty is the best policy!' We decided to take that to heart, and our business model today is to sell a lot of stuff at small profits. And the festival committee asked us to contribute some money this year, since we're participating and all—so when all's said and done, we're actually still in the red."

Honest to God, what has happened to this woman? When did she get so intelligent?

So it turned out the Axis Church still wasn't making a profit.

It was then that I remembered it had been my idea to have both churches contribute money to the festival.

"…Er, yeah. But y'know. Keep selling, and you'll be in the black in no time! I mean, look how popular you are! Actually, I'm surprised a church as poor as yours was able to come up with the money to participate in this festival in the first place!"

"I paid for that out of pocket. Don't you remember the bounty we got for beating the hydra? Between that and what was in my piggy bank, I made it work somehow. I wanted to build Emperor Zel a gorgeous dragonhouse, but I guess that can wait."

"……Oh—oh really?"

"What's wrong? If you're not feeling well, I can cast Heal on you. You've been working so hard lately, Kazuma, my friend. Here, just hold still. I'll whip up an especially powerful one just for you."

Then she smiled and Healed me with all her strength.

I was back in the council chamber, the second day of the festival safely concluded.

Talking to Aqua had opened my eyes.

She just genuinely wanted to enjoy the celebration. Compared with that, what did I want? To put salesgirls in swimsuits to indulge my own lust, to pit two churches against each other to make myself a little cash?

…I made up my mind.

I would tell Aqua everything that had gone on and apologize to everyone, quit my job as adviser, and enjoy the festival myself, starting tomorrow.

Yeah, tomorrow was the third day of the festival, when the fireworks display was planned. I would check it out with Megumin, lend an ear to the gripes of the long-suffering Darkness, and have a drink of wine with Aqua.

That was what was going through my mind as I opened the door, ready to announce my resignation...

"Ah, we've been waiting for you, esteemed adviser!"

"Take the seat of honor, sir!"

I entered the room and froze. The grinning committee members urged me to sit at the head of the table, but that wasn't what got my attention. My gaze was fixed on the other people in the room.

"Good evening, honored regular! The council members have just been telling us how hard you've been working."

"Thank you for your patronage, honored customer! We heard it was you who got the okay for people to dress up as succubi during this festival!"

Yep: It was two of the succubi who ran my favorite shop.

The president came up behind me where I stood frozen and gave me an encouraging squeeze of the shoulder as he sat me in a chair.

What was going on here? What was this? This was dangerous. It was very dangerous.

Specifically, what was dangerous was that the succubi weren't dressed the way they normally were.

This had to be their real appearances: one older succubus and one loli succubus, both dressed in sexy black bodysuits and wearing alluring smiles.

I still couldn't tear my eyes away from them as the president whispered to me. "I see you've met them before. These people run a small café here in town. As merchants in the downtown district, they supplied some of the salesgirls in swimsuits for the festival, and it seems they want to thank our adviser personally for getting them permission to dress that way..."

Uh... That would actually be kind of a problem.

After all, I'd just come in to say I was quitting as adviser.

I'd seen how hard Aqua was working. I had to be decisive.

If I entertained this meeting, I would just get carried away again.

Be strong, Kazuma Satou! Are you so easily swayed?!

Even when you're being thanked by sexy succubi?

"A festival calls for a drink, so let the two of us serve you. Heh-heh! You won't be going home tonight. You're one of our best customers, and we want to take good care of you!"

I grabbed a cup sitting nearby and let the older succubus, who had worked her way over to me, pour me a drink.

Then the president raised his glass.

"To the health of our honored adviser and to our continued sales! Let's have a toast from our adviser as well!"

I stood up, sandwiched between the two succubi, and proclaimed, "May we all have great happiness and even greater profits! Cheers!"

""""""Cheers!""""""

May There Be Shining Flowers in the Sky Tonight!

1

The third day of the festival.

I was asleep on my bed in my room when Megumin, wearing a dress and looking annoyed, said, "…You come home at dawn, and now you sleep so late? Come on—we are supposed to see the fireworks together today. Hurry up and get changed!"

I drank too much yesterday.

This world doesn't have a legal drinking age, so I'm sorry to say I've become rather acquainted with the taste of alcohol since coming here.

"Errgh, I'm afraid of what might happen if I go out in a big, noisy crowd of people right now…"

"You are the worst! Normally, when one has a date with a girl to go see fireworks, one tries to take it easy on the alcohol the day before. What were you even doing last night? You seemed in awfully high spirits when you came home."

There was no way I was going to tell her I had a succubus lady spoiling me rotten.

"Call Darkness… Get her to use her authority to move the fireworks display to tomorrow…"

"As much as I admire your refusal to actually abandon our date, I think continued selfish requests on your part are going to drive

Darkness insane. She already has her hands full with Aqua and the others today."

Wait, how's that again?

Last night, Aqua and her friends had seemed to be doing pretty well, so what happened?

As I lay there trying to think things through, Megumin tore the blankets off my bed and thrust my clothes into my hands…

"Yikes! W-wait a second—what are you doing?! Stop that; why are you trying to pull my clothes off?! You do the weirdest things sometimes!"

Nearly being stripped certainly woke me up.

"Your nakedness is hardly something to move me now, Kazuma. In the battle with the Kowloon Hydra, your clothes melted right off. Come on—if you aren't going to take your clothes off, then I'll do it myself."

The idea of being stripped naked by a girl wasn't entirely unpleasant, but I didn't want to think about what Aqua or Darkness would say if they saw us.

I got out of bed, changed my clothes in front of Megumin—who didn't even pretend to look away—and quickly washed my face and got ready.

"…I—I admit, even I didn't expect you to change in front of me so readily."

"I thought you weren't moved by my nakedness… Phew, that drink of water has me feeling a bit better. By the way, you said something about Aqua causing trouble. What's going on?"

"Yesterday, the Axis shop stalls did quite well for themselves, better than the Eris ones, in fact, and the Axis disciples are letting it go to their heads. Specifically, they claim the Axis Church should be granted more selling space because of their superior income."

I thought back to how Aqua had looked the day before.

Were the cracks starting to show already?

…No, no, it was too early to draw any conclusions—she had been reborn. She'd shown she could learn during the cicada hunt, and she had displayed such humility yesterday. Some of the Axis disciples must have gone rogue—that had to be it.

But…

"…I've got a bad feeling about this, so I think I'll let Darkness handle it. Yeah, I think I'll steer clear of the Axis booths today. Let's go see some fireworks."

Maybe Megumin had her suspicions, too, because she agreed immediately. "Indeed. It's a summer festival—why not take a break from unpleasant and dangerous things for a bit and go on a date?"

That's right: We finally had a summer festival here. I normally managed to get dragged into every fight and argument that came along, but surely I deserved to relax and enjoy the celebration—!

"—Somehow I kind of figured this would happen."

"Why the smart remark? Come on—hurry up." Megumin, looking perplexed, took my hand as I stood dejectedly at the entrance to the downtown district.

"Megumin, this is the first time I've ever gone to a festival or seen fireworks with anyone! I don't seem, like, weird or anything, do I?! I really tried to go all-out here!"

"There is nothing weird about you except that excitement. I am asking you, please, to try not to go to pieces at this festival of all places."

Megumin had set my heart fluttering with words like *date*, but then Yunyun came along.

I greeted Yunyun when she met us at the gate, then shuffled along behind the two girls, my shoulders slumped just a little…

"It is still a bit early to be alone with you. After the fireworks display, let's go home together."

Megumin whispered in my ear.

"In the past, I've always kept myself shut up in the house during festival time. To think the day would come when I could go enjoy a festival

like this—I'm so glad I left Crimson Magic Village! …Mr. Kazuma, what's wrong? You're behaving rather strangely…"

"Wha—? Huh?! I-i-i-it's nothing; I'm just excited about the festival! Say, Yunyun, why would you stay home when you could come to the festival and have a chance of running into a friend? I mean, as a high-level *hikikomori* myself, I understand the feeling. You don't go out to festivals or crowded places. Yeah, sounds like common sense when I put it that way."

Megumin's little ambush had put me into something of a panic, and Yunyun looked at me strangely.

"I'm not a *hikikomori* like you, Mr. Kazuma. I was afraid that if I went to the festival by myself and ran into all my classmates having fun there without me, they might pity me. I wouldn't be able to stand it if they were to say, *Oh, we're so sorry for not inviting you* or whatever else…"

"I get it—stop already! I was wrong. Just don't say any more! We'll keep you company today!"

Argh, dammit, what is it with me these days? I feel like Megumin permanently has the initiative.

And what's all this about going home together? She can't just mean going home, can she? She must have some "special event" in mind after that, right?

Is it okay for me to get my hopes up a little bit here?

Man, girls are no fair.

I mean, look how crazy she's made me just by whispering in my ear a little!

2

I'd had my way with the shooting gallery using my Deadeye skill and taken advantage of my immense Luck to bankrupt the lottery stall.

"…I think you should learn what it means to have mercy, Kazuma," Megumin said.

"She's right," Yunyun added. "The woman at the shooting gallery and the man at the lottery stall were both crying. They said they would have to close for the day."

I had been walking around and checking out the various shops with the two Crimson Magic Clan girls.

"Listen up, you two," I said. "Festivals are a battle against the shop-keepers. Back in my country, the people running the booths would show off some expensive item that you could 'win' if you were lucky enough, but they could sell every ticket and there still wouldn't be a winner. Or you'd win something and go home all excited, only to find out you'd won a clever fake."

"Sometime I want to sit down and properly hear about this country you're from, Kazuma," Megumin said. "…But I have to say, this year's festival does seem more fun than usual. Were you the one who suggested the costume parade? Everyone was really enjoying themselves, walking around in whatever costume they liked. I even saw some crazy people dressed up like succubi and incubi. I wouldn't be surprised to discover there were even some real ones wandering around."

I had to be careful; Megumin was proving sharper than I had anticipated. I looked around the festival.

Axel Town looked totally different from normal.

There was Vanir, selling masks at the world's creepiest mask shop. In among the succubi happily buying up his stock was Megumin; even she seemed to want a mask.

There was Yunyun, who had somehow gotten roped into helping Vanir.

It wasn't just demons enjoying the celebration: Animal people, short-eared elves, and dwarves—races you didn't see too much of around here—could all be found wandering about.

Bonfire light gave everything a fantastical look. I had never felt so much like I was in another world as I did today, I thought.

"This really is another world…"

* * *

Before I knew it, I found myself whispering the thought aloud.

"……"

Standing next to me, Megumin was watching me closely with a hint of concern, looking as if she wanted to say something.

"What? You look like you're trying to hold in an explosion."

"…Oh, it's nothing…"

Megumin, who would normally speak her mind regardless of whether she was talking to a king, a queen, or a general of the Demon King, was strangely reticent.

Maybe I should tell her sometime that I wasn't from this world.

Not that anything would come of it or that anything would change. She might just think I was crazy, like how Aqua could never get Megumin to believe her when she said she was a goddess.

Maybe it was because my life was newly stable, but there were times recently when I actually didn't think it was such a bad thing to have come to this world.

Maybe I really would tell her and the others about "my country" someday—

At that moment, though, a rumble I could feel in my bones came from the direction of Axel's reservoir.

The fireworks display had begun.

Flowers of every color burst in the sky above, accompanied by the *ooh*s and *ah*s of the crowd.

Megumin looked up at the sky. In what might have been an effort to shake the solemn atmosphere between us, she squeezed my hand gently…

"Kazuma, let's hurry over! If we don't get to the battle, we'll be too late!"

Her tender words perfectly suited the mood of…

"…Wait, battle? Hey, stop—don't pull! We can see the fireworks just fine from here!"

"What are you talking about? We're adventurers, aren't we? If we do not aid the defense now, who will protect the festival?!"

What was she talking about?

I was about to ask her when I saw the other adventurers in the area and stopped.

Everyone who looked remotely like a magic-user was dashing over. Even Yunyun, who had been there just a moment ago.

I chased after Megumin, shouting, "Hey, tell me what's going on! Seriously, what is this? Isn't this a fireworks display?! Where is everyone going?!"

"It's the bugs!" It wasn't Megumin but Yunyun who answered, running ahead of us.

"The bugs?! What about them? We build a bunch of bonfires during the festival, and they attract some insects—so what?!"

Megumin replied, "This happens every year. That's why they post that quest for the extermination of the insects. At night, the bugs from the nearby forest and plains are lured to the town by the firelight. They circle around overhead, looking for any chance to attack. That's what the fireworks display is for. We let off blasts and explosions right in the middle of them."

Um… Come again?

"Mr. Kazuma, I don't know what fireworks were for where you come from… But in our country, fireworks displays are a signal to go to war against encroaching insects!"

This stupid, stupid world!

3

I can't believe this.

After all that "let's be together" and whispering sweetly in my ear, Megumin was the first one in the moment the fireworks started.

Then, if you can believe it, the police stopped her from trying to set off a huge explosion right in the middle of town.

…And that meant she was dragged off to the station.

I knew she wasn't the most romantic person in the world, but you *could* take spoiling the mood too far.

The summer festival, the vibe in the air, had really gotten my hopes up. I wanted my poor feelings back.

After aiding in the defense against the bugs, I went back home—alone—and slunk off to my room.

But I couldn't just mope forever.

While I had been running around the battlefield like a chicken with its head cut off (we were at a festival—why would I bring my bow and arrows?), Chris found me, and we made a snap decision.

I dressed all in black and donned the weird mask.

I put the magic item I had bought just for this purpose in my backpack, and then everything was ready.

That's right: We were going to get our revenge on that nasty suit of armor.

Tonight, I was bringing a magical item that would help us against the shouting suit.

It was so late at night that it was practically the next day. Aqua still wasn't home—maybe she was out having fun at the festival—and I expected Darkness would soon be asleep.

My route to the meeting point with Chris went not through the front door but out the window of my own room. It would be trouble if anyone in the mansion happened to spot me sneaking around in black pajamas and a mask. Darkness would recognize me, and if she or especially Aqua found me, they would know immediately what I was going to do.

All right. Go time.

I lowered a rope out my window and was about to climb down it when…

"Kazuma. Your light is on; are you still up?"

I quickly pulled the rope back inside and shut the window.

"Y-y-yeah, I'm up, but I'm just about to go to sleep!" I said, stashing the rope as quickly as I could and making sure the door was locked. If she saw me in this getup, she would certainly ask where I was going.

"Okay... Um, I know it's late, but do you have a moment?"

Frankly, no, I didn't, but Darkness somehow sounded different from usual.

"...Yeah, fine. Just give me a second; I'm not presentable."

"Hrk?! S-sure, okay. Sorry I caught you at a bad time." Why did she sound a little panicked? I hurried to change my clothes. Then I stuffed the mask and my backpack into the closet.

"*Pant... Pant...* S-sorry to keep you waiting..."

"Sure, it's no— Hey, weren't you getting your clothes on? I won't ask what you were doing in there, but you could at least stop breathing hard!!" Darkness couldn't quite bring herself to look at me as I stood there panting.

Oops, I *was* in just my underpants.

...Hey, wait a second.

"Hold on—I wasn't doing anything, like, weird in here! Don't get the wrong idea!"

"F-fine, sure! Believe me, I won't, so just put on some clothes! And for the record, if you're going to do *that*, at least wash your hands!"

That's exactly the wrong idea I was talking about!

I wanted to clear up the misunderstanding, but I didn't have the time.

"...Ah, forget it. What do you want? You know, if you hang around outside my room dressed like that, Aqua's going to start spreading nasty rumors about you."

Darkness was wearing a thin negligee that left me unsure what to do with my eyes. If I hadn't been about to try to sneak out of the house to go pilfer a Sacred Treasure, I would have looked her up and down to my heart's content.

Of course, I did it anyway.

"S-so, um…are you just going to let me stand out here, or can I come in?"

There was something in my closet I definitely didn't want her to see, so I would have been happier to leave her in the hallway. But I could hardly say that, so instead I just sat down on my bed.

"What's up all of a sudden? Is it something that couldn't wait until morning?"

"Wh-what?! Well, uh, I guess maybe it could, technically, but… Well… You know, both of us have just been so busy recently, we don't even see each other much here at home, right?"

Darkness's half-baked attempt at an answer was accompanied by a nervous glance around my room as she settled uneasily on my bed. Her fingers worked restlessly for a moment before she seemed to find her nerve and looked up at me.

"Kazuma, I… I've apologized to you, but I haven't properly thanked you, so…I just wanted to take a moment when we were alone to say how grateful I am…" Her voice was quiet but firm, and she looked straight at me with a very serious expression.

Ah. Could she mean…?

"Is this about when I saved you from that lecherous lord? That was just something I decided to do on my own, and you don't need to thank me for it. I mean, you apparently took on our debts without mentioning it to anyone, but I never thanked you for that, right?"

I tried to sound lighthearted, but Darkness didn't look convinced.

While we were chatting, Chris was waiting for me.

What an annoying girl! I didn't need her to thank me.

I was fidgeting, almost hardly paying attention, when Darkness gave me a smile that made my heart ache, as if she might burst into tears at any moment. "You… You've shown me fun things and new things, things that were sad and things that made me angry—a wealth of emotions and experiences I never expected to have as a daughter of the nobility. If I'd never met you, I would never have traveled around with this party, never have gone on such amazing adventures. The year

since we met has been the most fun and the happiest time of my life."
She was practically whispering.

As I sat there completely lost for what to say, Darkness took my
hand in both of hers. "So please, let me thank you. Not just for saving
me from Alderp's clutches. Thank you for staying friends with a girl
who everyone else starts avoiding as soon as they find out who she really
is. I love living here with you and the others. It's like... Yes, I don't even
know my dearly departed mother's face, but I think if she had lived, I
would have known this feeling s-sooner..."

She was starting to stutter, as if she was feeling shy.

"That's why I want to thank you now. For always being with me.
For rescuing me when I had even given up on myself. Thank you from
the bottom of my heart..."

Darkness suddenly switched to the more elaborate tone of a noble,
but she was still holding my hand, and now she squeezed it gently.

I thought my heart might burst from sheer nerves.

What was going on here? Why had this "love event" come on so
suddenly?

Hadn't I been going down the Megumin route? I thought we had
been feeling pretty cozy, that I was more or less settled on that branch,
and then suddenly here comes the "noblewoman path."

Even I thought I was hardly making sense at this point.

What the heck; why is this happening?!

*No, wait! Calm down—take it easy, Kazuma Satou. She's just thank-
ing you. You're not a virgin; what are you getting all nervous for?*

Hold on—I am a virgin!

*More to the point, I can't get carried away here, not if you think about
it sensibly; I mean, Megumin and I were enjoying the fireworks just earlier and feeling pretty good about ourselves, and now I'm getting in good
with Darkness on the very same day, and if someone were to say,* You're

something else, Kazuma, *I wouldn't be able to deny it because no wait that's not the point!*

What am I even thinking I'm so confused I just wait wait wait this is no time to panic; this is Darkness we're dealing with, Darkness who always says the weirdest things, Darkness who gets ticked off at the drop of a hat, Darkness with whom I very nearly crossed that last and final line…

"So I… Tonight, see, I… Uh… I wanted to thank you…"

Darkness, who was blushing, Darkness whose face was drawing closer to mine, Darkness who was licking her lips because maybe they were dry, yes, that's the Darkness we were talking about, Kazuma Satou, and now you've come this far, so show that you're a man!

I just needed to be cool and take the lead, really go for it:

"D-d-don't m-mention it; Megumin thanked me once when we were alone together for helping you, too, and you know it's all good; I mean, we're buddies, right?!"

Okay, that wasn't quite as cool as I'd hoped, but I'd give myself eighty out of one hundred there. *Let's just keep really going for it.*

"…Geez, you bring up Megumin at a time like this? Some guys really know how to kill a moment."

Okay, not going. Darkness stood up, a mixture of annoyance and disappointment on her face.

"But speaking of her, we got word from the police. They said she would be released late tonight. I guess it was cruel of me to try to be in your room right when they were letting her out…"

As she spoke, Darkness leaned over toward me.

Her lips brushed my cheek ever so gently.

Then she stood up again, biting her lip. "That was the kiss on the cheek I promised you for beating the Kowloon Hydra," she said. "I'll have to thank you for saving me from Alderp some other time…!"

As I watched her go, I started shouting. "The hellllll, Darkness?! Wait! You can't get me this fired up and then leave me with a stupid kiss on the cheek! You, Megumin, everyone around here just likes to get a guy's hopes up! I want a do-over! A do-over, do you hear me?! I know you've got it in you—just muster up that courage and take the next step!"

"I truly cannot fathom what is wrong with you! I want our moment back!"

4

Darkness stormed angrily back to her room, and I buried myself under my covers to try to get some sleep. Then I realized I had completely forgotten about Chris and rushed out to our agreed-upon meeting point, two hours after we had agreed to meet there.

When I arrived, there was Chris, wearing black clothes and a mask over her face just like I was.

"You are so late!" she exclaimed. "What could possibly have taken so long?!"

"Uh, sorry, there was some stuff with Darkness. I never thought she would come to my room so late at night and looking like *that*..."

"Huh?!" Chris went from angry to stiff. "J-just wait a second. You won't make me forget about being upset that easily. You're playing this up, but I'm sure nothing serious happened, right?"

"I mean, I guess not. Darkness just suddenly kissed me is all."

"Guh?!" Chris gasped, shattering her facade of detached cool, her face frozen in shock.

I didn't think a goddess was ever supposed to look that way.

"As amusing as I find that face, we're running out of time," I said. "I don't know if it's because of what happened, but physically, I'm feeling pretty good tonight."

"Whaaaaa—?! Hey, hold on. How can you get kissed and still be so calm?! You were joking, weren't you? Come on—you were pretending, right?!"

Chris was really bent on this for some reason.

"No, it's true. You can ask Darkness. Ask her, 'Is it true that you came to Kazuma's room in the middle of the night and suddenly kissed him?' I wonder what's been going on anyway. Just the other day, Megumin was talking about how she, y'know, *likes* me. In fact, today she said we should go home together after the fireworks display—not that we got to, thanks to her spoiling that moment. What do I do, Chief? I might take my next step into adulthood during the festival."

"What, seriously?! Come to think of it, you did mention something the other day about how you were feeling pretty good about things with Megumin and how Darkness seemed to be noticing you, too. W-wait just a second—do you have a love triangle on your hands here?!" Chris clapped her hands over her mouth, then looked at me with undisguised interest. "Oh wow... When did Darkness get so bold?! Wait a second. Did you say Megumin likes you, too? So what are you going to do?! Who are you going to choose?!"

"Hey, hey, don't rush me. I don't exactly have this figured out myself yet. This sort of thing happens all the time in manga and novels in Japan. All the pretty girls you meet fall in love with you; you start up a harem... The thing is, I've got no complaints about either of their looks, but you know what they're like on the inside. Plus, the way these scenarios go, I'll probably trip the flags for some more girls along the way, so it's a little early to start making any choices. Tell me, Chief, what do you think I should do?"

"I'm starting to think maybe you should just drop dead... I have to admit I'm surprised, though. When did things get this way between you all...?"

Maybe goddesses were immune to talk of love, or maybe she was shocked to discover that her friend Darkness was suddenly going to step into adulthood before she was, but in any event, I was reduced to dragging the dizzy Chris along behind me as we headed for Undyne's house.

It was a cloudless night, a beautiful full moon in the sky.

There was a reason we had decided so abruptly to go thieving tonight of all nights.

No doubt the mansion would be on alert after our last break-in. But with the festival going on, we assumed they would let their guard down just a little bit. Tonight, however, was the night following the fireworks display. Nobles had a responsibility to protect the town, and the guards at this mansion had been among those sent to the battle.

That meant they would be good and tired, and given that this festival came but once a year, there was also a good chance there would be some drunken partying going on. I still had my little plan to deal with the yelling armor, but if my idea should fail and we were to be pursued, we would simply remove our black suits and masks and fade away into the crowd.

—When we finally got to Undyne's house, we found that the back entrance through which we'd snuck last time was completely blocked off, and the only other way in—the front gate—was watched by two guards. Chris told me that ever since our attempted heist, the gate had been watched all night, every night.

We were observing the mansion from a distance and discussing our options.

"So what do we do now, Lowly Assistant? This place isn't as big as the royal castle. A few guards really could be a pain."

"Good question—I'd like to distract them and sneak in if possible…"

"Uh, um… Are you two, by any chance, members of the Silver-Haired Thief Brigade?"

The voice was very sudden and very right behind us. I sucked in a breath and turned around.

"P-p-p-pleased to meet you!" the newcomer said. "Er, although we aren't really meeting at all, at least not for the first time! I encountered you at the royal castle once… I'm, well, I suppose you could call me a fan of yours. I'm the Arch-wizard Megumin!"

I'd thought the police had detained her—but there was Megumin in the flesh.

5

For the life of me, I couldn't tell you how this happened.

"Wow, we're famous already! I mean, famous enough to get a two-hundred-million-eris bounty on our heads, I guess!!"

Chris seemed at once embarrassed and elated to be told Megumin was a fan of hers. I wanted to point out that this was not the time to be so self-conscious, but I was more interested in wrapping this up without getting in trouble.

Chris and I were both speaking in manufactured voices, but a sharp-enough listener would probably be able to tell who we were. Megumin, however, was too excited for that.

"For a thief gang to earn a bounty on their heads, that's really amazing! Oh yeah, I wanted to ask you: When you broke into the castle, was it because you knew the princess possessed a dangerous Sacred Treasure and you wanted to protect her?!"

"Oh, uh, yes, that's right," I said. "We're what the world calls righteous thieves. Normally, we're on the side of the common people, but we can't ignore a woman in danger, even if she is a princess. Wherever people are in trouble, whether noble mansion or royal castle, we'll sneak right in. That's us, the Masked Thief Brigade."

"Oh, wooow…!"

I had to admit, the envious way Megumin was looking at me felt pretty good.

"H-hang on, Lowly Assistant—aren't we the Silver-Haired Thief Brigade?! No fair changing our name. I'm the chief, remember?!"

"You're one to talk about unfair, Chief. Remember how when

things were going south in the castle, you said we should call it the Masked Thief Brigade and I could be chief?!"

We briefly ignored Megumin and her glittering eyes while we had a sidebar.

"So what are you doing here?" Megumin asked. "This is a noble's house, is it not? …One who is not known for his decency, at that…" She looked even more expectant than before.

I looked at Chris, and she looked at me, and then we both nodded.

"Megumin… That was your name, right? As it happens, we're after a certain object that resides in this house. An object crucial to the future of mankind. Thievery is never an activity to be praised, but… But this is something we must do—yes, even if it puts a bounty on our heads."

"Wow… Wooow…!" Megumin looked at us like we were genuine heroes.

"It's true: We're about to break into that house," Chris added. "And we're going to get ourselves a trump card to use against the Demon King's army. If you feel you need to tell the police, we won't stop you… But I hope you'll believe us when we say that this is for the sake of all humanity!"

"Yes! Yes, I believe you! And of course I won't report you!" Megumin assured us. "But…in exchange, let's say, there's something I'd like to ask." She was fidgeting, looking weirdly shy. Then she bowed her head and gave us a letter. "Please read this! It's a fan letter I wrote describing how cool and attractive you both are! I've been keeping it with me at every moment, in hopes that we might meet again someday!!"

Come to think of it, I did remember her saying she wanted to give a letter to the thieves after we got back from the capital.

Actually, my heart was pounding to get this letter. Megumin thought she was just writing to the heroes she was so enamored of, but for me it was sort of like getting a love letter.

I was about to take the letter carefully when—

"Thank you, young lady; I'll read this with great interest when this job is over."

—Chris grabbed it instead.

"Hold it, Chief! She was giving that to me!"

"I don't think so. Megumin was giving a fan letter to the Silver-Haired Thief Brigade, okay?! It's not addressed to *you*; it's to both of us, so it's only right that the chief should take it!"

As we began fighting as quietly as we could over the letter, Megumin bowed to us again. "Thank you so very much for accepting it. There was something I was looking forward to after the fireworks display, but unfortunately, things didn't go as planned, and I was feeling down… But thanks to you, tonight wasn't all bad."

Then she gave us an innocent smile.

6

"It's a good thing we made it through that without being discovered, Chief. But I can't tell if running into someone like that at this late hour is good luck or bad."

"Between the both of us, I don't think we can have bad luck. We even got a fan letter out of it."

Megumin had left us, saying that she wished she could help somehow but that she had to hurry home and apologize to someone. Then she had said good-bye, but we could still see her taking little worried glances back at us.

Could the "someone" she had to apologize to possibly be me?

"Chief, do you think I could go home for today? I bet I could score a Megumin event by being at my place when she got there."

"You certainly may *not* go home. This is the perfect night to break in! What do you mean by 'Megumin event' anyway?! At least choose between Megumin and Darkness!"

It looked like I wasn't going to get out of this. *We'd better make this quick, then.*

At that moment, I noticed Chris trying to pack the fan letter away close to her chest.

"...Chief, what say we have a little contest to see who gets to keep that letter when this job is over?"

"Okay, a simple battle of rock, paper, scissors."

"Nothing luck based!"

The unexpected turn of events had made it necessary to get back home as soon as possible. I wanted to wrap this up pronto.

"Let's overpower the guards here," I said. "I feel like I'm at the top of my game tonight—two guards? No sweat. I'll wipe 'em out in the blink of an eye." Maybe it was my improving standing with Darkness and Megumin that inspired such boldness in me.

"What are you, a monster?" Chris asked. "I remember you were the same way when we were breaking into the royal castle, all excited. The wee hours of the night seem to really invigorate you somehow."

"If that's what you think, then pretty much every NEET in Japan is a monster. We want to get as close as we can without being noticed, so activate your Ambush skill, Chief. It's a full moon tonight, and they keep bonfires burning throughout the festival, so it's plenty bright. We'll have to be extra-careful."

Chris and I used our Ambush skills as we slid along the wall like ninjas, closing in on the guards. The two men were chatting amicably, without a hint of concern. If we could get the drop on them, everything would proceed as planned.

Trying to judge my timing, I listened in on what they were saying.

"Man, this year's festival has been the best! It's been really exciting, and you've got the Axis Church and everything. And those salesgirls in swimsuits. That was a stroke of genius."

"The succubus cosplay thing is a big part of it, too. I saw the most *incredible* chicks, man. I'm just loving this festival. Hey, did you hear? I guess this year they've got somebody orchestrating the entire event."

Ooh, could that be yours truly?

The fact that even soldiers were talking about this stuff meant I had really done a good job.

"I think I know who you mean. You're talking about that guy who came up with the devious idea to pit the Eris and Axis Churches against each other and let them juice up the whole festival, right?"

"Yeah, that's the one. Getting the Axis Church involved, the succubus cosplay, the swimsuits, he thought of all of it. I think his name was—"

I jumped from the shadows.

The two panicked guards reached for their swords—

"*Drain Touch!*"

—but I slapped a hand over each of their mouths and drained their magical energy. Before the two guys could deliver their very unfavorable information in front of Chris, they both quickly fell silent.

"Wh-whoa, now, Lowly Assistant, don't go too crazy! Though I suppose I am glad you took them by surprise. It did seem like they were about to cry out."

"I decided that with the form I'm in tonight, I could do it. And I did, didn't I? Don't worry—just leave it to me."

Actually, it had been a pretty close call.

Sure, the guards might have been about to shout, but if they had gotten another word out, I might have been in for some real divine punishment.

Chris dragged the two unconscious guards into the bushes. "I'm glad it turned out well, but be careful next time, okay? After having to go out and fend off the bug attack this evening, everyone here will be tired, careless. We won't get another chance like this."

"I know that. So let's hurry up, 'cause I wanna head home and flirt with Megumin."

"Weren't you in a good place with Darkness just before you came here? If you get yourself stabbed one of these days, don't come whining to me, okay? And I won't be granting you any more resurrections if that's how you get yourself killed—you hear me?"

I wish she wouldn't say such unsettling things.

But I was going to be fine; it wasn't like either of them had asked me to go out with them. So it didn't matter what I did with whom; they couldn't complain.

"But you know," Chris went on, "what those guards said kind of bugs me… About there being an orchestrator for this festival or whatever. Do you know anything about that, Lowly Assistant?"

"M-me? Not a thing…"

…Now I had a whole new reason for wanting to get this job over with.

Our second break-in to Undyne's mansion was going as smoothly as the first. It helped that we now knew the layout of the house. Still, the fact that things had gone *this* well without any hiccups had to be related to the fact that I was with the goddess of good fortune herself.

I hated to consider the possibility, but if I hadn't tripped that alarm in the vault at the royal castle, things might have gone just as easily there.

At length, we reached the same treasure room we had before. Standing in front of the hidden door, we nodded at each other.

I pulled what would be our key item this time out of my pocket, then pushed open the secret door. As we entered the room, before Aigis had time to shout, I flung on the ground the crystal I had bought at the magic-item shop.

When the crystal shattered, a special barrier surrounded the room.

This was an item I had purchased not at Wiz's shop, but at another magic-item place that sold things that were actually useful.

What I had gotten was a magic crystal that temporarily put up a weak spirit barrier. It should prevent Aigis's telepathy from traveling beyond this room.

Chris came in after me, reaching into her backpack to pull out something else we had gotten at the magic-item shop, a cloth wrapping with a mild magic-blocking effect. We would wrap Aigis in it to prevent him from using his telepathy at all.

<I wondered who could be bursting in here—if it isn't the cat-burglar twins! You don't take a hint very well, do you? C'mere, everyone! Get 'em!>

Aigis started shouting the moment he saw us. I ignored him, loosening the chains that held him in place.

<Hey, what are you—? You think you've got time for that?! A big, bad noble owns this house. If he catches you, it's the death penalty, y'hear me? ...Hey, it's awfully quiet out there. What's going on?>

"Ha! You think we'd just wander back in here without a plan?" I said. "Your telepathy won't reach the rest of the house. Too bad for you!" I laughed nastily, letting Aigis know that this was payback for last time.

<What have you done?! Hey, stop, okay?! Parley! I demand parley!! You want my power, right?! Okay, if you find me a suitable owner, then I'll cooperate with you! I'm willing to compromise on who it is; just work with me here!!>

Aigis was begging us now; his flippant attitude had vanished. I removed another chain.

"Too bad you didn't say that the last time we were here, dumbass! I guarantee your next owner will be a man! A big, burly, macho type, so *steel* yourself!"

<Don't screw with me, kid! Stoppit! Just imagine if you were a sentient suit of armor! You wouldn't want to be worn by some stinky dude, would you? Wouldn't you rather defend a gorgeous young woman?!>

"I sympathize, believe me, but you have no idea what you've put us through. Don't expect us to go out of our way to accommodate you, jerk!"

"L-Lowly Assistant, I know I'm in no position to judge, having argued with the armor last time, but you don't sound very adult..." Chris backed away a little at the sight of me fighting with this inanimate object far more viciously than she ever had.

<Ahhhhh! Nooo, nooooo! A woman! If someone has to wear me, I want it to be a woman! I don't care if she's a black-haired beauty or a golden-locked loli or a sexy redhead; any of them would be fine as long as she was female! Don't you understand? Whoever wears me gets all sweaty in battle, and who wants that to be some guy?!>

I had to admit I felt a twinge of empathy for the screeching Aigis. Covering the body of some filthy, clammy dude was a pretty unpleasant punishment, but...

"Give it up already," I said. "And by the way, making a scene on the way home won't get you anywhere, okay? Chris there has some coverings that prevent weak magic from getting through. We're going to wrap you in them to get you out of here. Speaking of which, you're awfully demanding for an inanimate object. Selfishness and immobility don't go well togeth—"

As I spoke, I removed the last of Aigis's chains.

<Grrrahhh!>

An impact on my chin set my head spinning.

"L-Lowly Assistant?! W-wait just a second! How are you moving?!"

I tried to listen to Chris while also grasping my wobbling head to steady it. I looked at Aigis, struggling to comprehend what was happening, when—

<I've decided. I'm going on a journey. A journey to find the beautiful woman who can wear me. As much as I enjoyed my life here, being waxed by the maids every day, it's always possible more clowns like you will show up. I'm going to find my own master.>

What greeted my eyes was Aigis, now free of his chains, gently shadowboxing.

And also talking crazy.

Chris said desperately, "Wait just a minute, Aigis; this world needs your power! If you like, maybe *I* could wear you until we find you a new master..."

<Fuuuck that! As if I would enjoy covering some thief who I can't even tell if they're a guy or a girl! I told you—I'm going to find my own

master for myself, all right?! …If you really want, though, I could go down the checklist to see how compatible we are… Hmm, face: A rank. Job compatibility: C rank. I'm not even going to bother ranking your chest. Sorry, but it's gonna be a 'no' from me…>

"Grrr! I thought maybe you'd work with me if I played nice! But if that's how you want to do this, we can use force! *Bind*!!"

Chris had finally had enough. She flung the wire she kept at her hip at him. She was going to stop Aigis—!

<Ooh, whatcha gonna do with that? You wanna tie me up? Boy, the cuties always turn out to be freaks in bed!>

Except she didn't. The wire fell limply to the ground.

Aigis raised both hands and shrugged in a *What can ya do?* gesture, mocking Chris openly.

"*Bind*!!"

I activated the same skill, but my wire dropped to the ground, too.

<Sure, just keep tryin', kid. Don't you get it yet? What do you take me for? I'm the legendary sacred armor Aigis, remember? The strongest, most magic-resistant, most skill-neutralizing, owner-healing, singin-gest, dancingest armor in the world. A couple of cut-rate pickpockets like you don't have what it takes to beat me!>

What a jerk!

"Okay, Chief, I guess skills don't work on him, but if they could hold him with chains, it must mean he's not as strong as all that! Let's pin him down and tie him up!"

"R-right! I'll come from the right; you come from the left!"

Aigis adopted what almost looked like a karate pose. <Ooh, still wanna come at me? I'm the master of the iron fist—literally! My entire body is a weapon!>

"Does this guy ever shut up?!" I exclaimed. "I've never heard armor squeak so loud! Grrrahhh!"

Chris and I both jumped at Aigis at once, grabbing on to his torso.

"Okay, got him!" Chris said.

"Chief, let's pull his arms clean off! Break him into pieces and stuff him in your backpack! If it looks like trouble, we could just leave the helmet here in this room!"

<Hey, watch your mouth. My beautiful body doesn't have a single seam, so you can't break it apart—my master has to say a magic phrase when they put me on. If you want to carry me out of here, maybe wearing me would be the fastest way. The phrase is 'I'm gonna be an armored girl, tee-hee!' Go ahead—say it.>

"I-I'm gonna be an armored—"

"Chief, there's no way that stupid phrase is the magic key; he's just tricking you! Whoa, h-hey, this guy's surprisingly strong...!"

Aigis was trying to leave the room, dragging both of us along with him...!

"Chief, this is bad! If he gets out of the room, we won't be able to block his telepathy!"

"Argh, c'mon—Aigis, for goodness' sake! I'm Eris. The goddess responsible for this world! It's my duty to oversee you, so please just come along quietly!"

<Yeah, okay, sure. Pleased to meetcha... What a shame—you've got such a cute face. But what's inside matters, too. I'll try to keep that in mind as I look for my master.>

"Ex*cuse* me?!"

Chris was enraged not to be recognized as a real goddess.

<Anyway, kids, it looks like this is where we say good-bye. If you want me so badly, sweetheart, first make yourself pretty enough to stop a man in his tracks. Work on that bust, especially. I know there are some guys out there who *say* they go gaga over a flat chest, but if you ask me, that's loser talk.>

"Grrrgh!" Chris clung to Aigis's arm, red up to her ears, but the armor just walked out the door, dragging us along behind him.

<Hey, everyone here at House Undyne—yeah, the ones who couldn't even protect *me*, the world's greatest treasure. It's been nice

hanging with y'all! Sorry I didn't get a chance to ask first, but I'm heading out to find my master. If you want me back, get a girl ready, and make sure she's a hottie! That's when you'll see me again!>

The telepathy echoed throughout the entire house, strong enough to make my head hurt.

<Whoo-hoo! I'm free! Free as I've ever been! Today, I might as well be a bird! Aigis Kick!!>

Aigis shook us loose, ran out of the treasure room, and then jumped out a window that had to be at least three stories up.

He had hardly finished jumping before lights started going on all over the house, and we heard shouting. The commotion he made had obviously woken up the household.

"What's going on?! Are there thieves again?!"

"That was Aigis's voice! Check the treasure room!"

Crap, they'd be coming this way!

Last time, we had torn the curtain off the window across from the vault and used it as a rope to escape. But maybe to stop the same thing from happening again, the curtain hadn't yet been replaced.

"Chief, we're in deep here. We're on the third floor with no way out. I move that we tie your Bind wire to that pillar and use it to climb down!"

"You have a wire, too, Lowly Assistant. Maybe we should use yours!"

"Mine is a super-expensive special-order wire! If they traced it, they could find me!"

"Is that why you were so keen to get it back when you failed to Bind Aigis?! Well, mine's special-order, too—extra-light. They'll find us for sure!"

"Brace yourself, Chief. It's been a while since I got really serious, but I think now's the time." Then I steadied my breathing.

"It's not time to panic yet," Chris said. "It's all right; I'll manage something. Don't forget who I am. I'm the goddess of good fortune, right?"

Chris gave me a mischievous smile, and that was when it happened.

There was a flash from outside, and at the same time, every window in the Undyne household shattered.

Along with the tinkling of glass came a roar that echoed throughout the summer night—a sound any inhabitant of our town would recognize immediately.

7

This was all the fault of that obnoxious armor.

"Kazuma, come out! If you get out here right now, I can still let you off with a stern lecture!"

Darkness was kicking furiously at the other side of the door.

"How uncouth, Young Lady! If you wish to call yourself a young woman of the nobility, can you not conduct yourself with more restraint?!"

I was leaning against the door as hard as I could, trying to prevent her from kicking it down.

"Sure, this is the *one* time you want to treat me like a noble! Kazuma, get out here and explain yourself! Otherwise, Chris here will have to take your share of the punishment all by herself!"

"Lowly Assistant, help meee!!"

I could hear Chris's voice on the other side of the door. But…

"Sorry, Darkness, but that trick won't work on me. Sure, that was Chris's voice. But the chief I know and trust would never let herself be captured so easily. You had Aqua cast her party-trick magic on you so you could imitate Chris's voice, didn't you? Don't underestimate my powers of deduction. That was *you* speaking just now!"

"What are you talking about, Lowly Assistant?! You don't *have* powers of deduction!!"

Chris's pained voice tried to counter my flawless logic.

I was currently holed up at an inn.

After Aigis's breakout, Chris and I had slipped past the household staff, all shaken by the explosion, and after being pursued around town, we had ducked into a random inn...

Darkness's voice came again from beyond the door I was bracing myself against. "Kazuma, you can come out now! It's just Chris and me, no police, nobody from Undyne's house! Come on, your 'chief' or whatever is in big trouble—can you just leave her out here?"

I said only:

"Do what you like."

"Traitor!" Chris's voice exclaimed. "Come on, Darkness—untie these ropes! I'll help you drag my lowly assistant out of there!"

"H-hey, are you really...?!"

One hour later.

Darkness had kicked down my door and taken me captive; now I sat, feet tucked under my behind, alongside Chris, whose upper body was bound with ropes.

"So—tell me again why you did this. I told you before that if you would just explain what was going on, I could talk to people. Damn it all. The Undyne household got a good look at both of you, so now every adventurer in town, and others besides, are looking high and low for you so they can claim your bounty."

Darkness, who had given us a more or less fair hearing, was rubbing her temples as if she had a headache.

Chris and I were both still tied up, so we had to use our chins to point at each other.

"I said we should ask you, Darkness," I said. "'Darkness can use her influence to get the armor for us,' I said. But the chief here—"

"Huh?! Yes, I admit you said that, Lowly Assistant! But, Darkness, that noble came into possession of the Sacred Treasure by illegal means, and he's not known for being a nice guy, and I was sure he would just play dumb if you asked him about it! And you were so busy being governor!"

Darkness heaved a very long, very deep sigh. "However busy I was, I would have made time for you if it would have prevented you from committing a crime. And even if Undyne did get the armor illegally, nobles have their ways. If you offer them enough compensation, the profit motive usually takes over. And *that*...!"

"Ow, ow, ow, ow! Darkness, stop! I'm sorry—I'll be sure to ask you next time before I steal something!"

"*Not* stealing is always an option, you know!" Darkness, furious, was pinning Chris's temples between her fists. "Do you want to know what makes me angriest, though?" She fixed me with a piercing glare. "After what happened between you and me last night, you just wandered off to go thieving—that's hardest of all to forgive! You could afford to act a *little* conflicted!! Think about how you behaved after that and imagine how I suffered from humiliation...!"

"Aaaaaaghhh, it's gonna break! You're gonna crack my skull! I'm sorry; I'm so sorry; I was wrong! But if you were going to be so embarrassed, you shouldn't have done something like that in the first place! You just kiss a guy and then stop halfway—I wasn't exactly feeling great, either!"

Darkness had me in a hawk-talon grip, and I thought my head was about to cave in...!

"Pfwah!"

That was when Chris suddenly made a very strange noise. Then she started to tremble, just enough that it was almost audible...

"Whoawhoawhoawhoa... So all that stuff you were saying last night, Lowly Assistant—it was true...?! It really happened?! Darkness *did* give you a kiss?!"

"Huh?! Chris, I don't think that matters right now! Wait—Kazuma, you even told her about *that*?!"

"What else was I supposed to do? She wouldn't leave me alone about why I was late! Anyway, after everything you and I have done together, I think it's a little late to be embarrassed over a kiss! You've even washed my back in the bath, and we've both seen each other naked. Hell, when I broke into your mansion, *you* were the one who suggested we become adults together!"

"Ahhhh, Kazumaaaaaaa! Fine, I get it; let's end this conversation right now—this isn't the time for this anyway! Here, I'll untie your bindings, so let's just get out of here, and both of you try to help!"

Darkness was glowing red as she hurried to undo the ropes.

"I think I just heard something really incredible. Will someone *please* tell me what's going on?! Have you two really gone that far?! Am I the only child here?!"

"We can talk about that later, Chris! Here, I'll untie you, too…"

"Later, my foot! I need details! Come on, Darkness—why won't you tell me? What happened to our friendship as women?!"

I rubbed my wrists where the bindings had been as I observed the two girls, positions now thoroughly reversed.

"Y-you don't give up, do you, Chris? I told you—it doesn't matter! Sheesh! You and Aqua and Megumin—why do all of you have to decide to cause trouble right when I'm the acting governor?" Darkness began rubbing her temples again.

"…Huh?" I said. "You mean I'm not the only one? Aqua and Megumin did something, too?"

"…Megumin is currently confined in a holding cell at the police station. Apparently, she cast explosion magic in town last night for no reason at all. I asked her again and again why she did it, but all she would say was 'I never got to use my magic at the fireworks display, and I just wanted to let it out. I think my explosion magic was most beautiful of all, and I shall not repent, but I will pay for damages.' I could hardly understand what she was talking about. I decided to let the police keep her until the festival is over."

The origin of the shock wave that had assaulted the Undyne household the night before had, of course, been Megumin. She had continued to look nervously back over her shoulder as she left us, and when she saw the lights go on in the house, she realized our theft had failed and, assuming we were in trouble, had used her magic.

Then she had fallen over, immobile from using up all her MP, and was promptly arrested.

I felt bad for her and resolved to make it up to her sometime.

"Okay, so what about Aqua? What did she do?"

Darkness frowned as if she didn't want to answer that question.

"Those Axis Church followers... They made so much more money at this festival than anticipated that...starting next year, they want to fund the entire celebration and make it solely the Aqua Appreciation Festival."

Chapter 5

May There Be a Legend for This Beginner Town!

1

"All right, Aqua, tell me what's going on here!"

At the Axis Church on the outskirts of town.

I'd heard that festival preparations for tonight were being done there, so I ran over to find Aqua enjoying a drink with Cecily, and I lit into her.

"Oh, Kazuma, what's got you so worked up?" Aqua had a wineglass in her hand, and on her knee sat her chick, which she was petting like she was the villain in some movie.

Beside her was Cecily, who was acting like a maid serving her mistress.

"Ha-haaa, you can smell a party from a mile away, can't you, Kazuma? Well, I won't argue if you want to join us. You may not be an Axis follower, but you have worked really hard for this festival. Come on—sit here beside me. I'll share some of my fresh-made *yakisoba* with you." She pushed a dish toward me, carefree as anything.

"You idiot!" I said. "This isn't the time to be eating *yakisoba*! What the hell is going on here?!"

I thrust out the application request Darkness had given me.

"Oh, hey, that's the application I submitted. 'One: We request that starting next year, the name of the festival be changed to the Aqua Appreciation Festival and the Eris Church be barred from participation. Two: We request that the laws regarding gelatinous slime be relaxed...' Hey, I don't remember writing this second thing."

"I wrote that, Lady Aqua!" Cecily said. "I worked so hard for this festival that I thought maybe I could get a reward!"

"I see. That sounds good. So what seems to be the problem?"

"It is not *good*! And it's all problems! I'm asking what exactly this is!"

While I stood there enraged, Aqua had a whispered conference with Cecily beside her.

"Huh, I wonder what Kazuma is so upset about. Is it because he wasn't invited to our victory celebration?"

"I don't think so, milady. It's because we didn't ask him what he wanted when we submitted our requests."

Aqua listened carefully to what Cecily was saying, then scribbled something on the application and handed it back to me.

Three: We request that hereafter, all salesgirls at the festival shall wear swimsuits.

"What are you, stupid?! That's not what I'm upset about! And after all that talk about not getting carried away and honestly trying your best! Then you go and pull a stunt like this?!"

"Waaaaah!! What are you doing? I added your request to the list!"

I was tearing up the application when Cecily got in between Aqua and me. "Now just a minute. What do you mean by letting Our Lady's compassion go to waste? I, Cecily, humbly declare in the name of the Axis Church that I will shove my way through your front door every night, endlessly singing Axis hymns!"

"I'd like to see you try! You've taken everyone for fools! I oughta knock some sense into both of you!"

"Wh-what? How can you say that after we worked so hard? Surely we're entitled to a little relaxation! Cecily said it! She said, 'Lady Aqua, you are Our Lady, and you deserve to live your life at the height of comfort while everybody fawns over you. I'm going to devote the full power of the Axis Church to making life easy for you from now on'!"

"You just met her the other day, and she's already got that kind of control over you? Come on—we're going home! I don't want you seeing this weirdo anymore! And you, don't make Aqua any more worthless than she already is!"

"'This weirdo'?!"

Aqua slipped out of my grasp and hid behind Cecily, who was still frozen in shock.

"I'm not going home until after the festival," Aqua said. "In fact, I'm not going home at all! …Being so smart, I've learned something. I've learned that here, they worship me! And by the way, Kazuma, now that we've made this festival such a huge success, there's no way they'll want to go without an Aqua Appreciation Festival next year. Just you go have a look at Eris's precious festival! *Our* booths get more and more visitors by the day, but who goes to *their* booths? Crickets, that's who!"

Here I had been thinking that for once, things might actually turn out well, but now I found out that Aqua hadn't changed a bit. She had been acting so different lately that I'd wondered if she had eaten something strange, but deep down, she was still the same.

I wanted to take back how impressed I had been at her growth and maturity, and at the same time, I was a little disgusted with myself to discover I was actually kind of relieved to know that the status quo remained intact.

Cecily proudly picked up the theme. "Lady Aqua is right. With our shops as popular as they are, the Eris Church can't hope to come back. And…don't think you're the only one with a flair for business. Our Lady Aqua still has a secret plan up her sleeve!"

A secret plan? There had to be something fishy there; I was sure of it.

2

I wandered around town, the Axis Church building safely behind me, brainstorming a fitting punishment for those girls.

Aqua and her church were getting ornery because they thought they had made the festival a success all by themselves. So maybe I should ally myself with the Eris followers and come up with some new shop ideas?

...Nah. I was all out of million-dollar ideas, and I would have my hands full with even just one or two new shops.

Well, I've got no choice. Maybe I should poke my head in at the Eris Church.

When I got there, I found...

"Ah, Lowly Assistant, how'd it go?"

...Chris, sweeping the area in front of the church with a broom. By the tone of her voice, she was well aware of how I had burst into the Axis Church practically foaming at the mouth.

"It didn't," I said. "I couldn't even talk with them... They just don't learn unless they get burned... What should I do? This is really my fault for even getting Aqua and her friends' permission to be part of the festival in the first place. I want to give those idiots something to think about before this situation is too far gone to salvage."

I was more than half-serious, but Chris shook her head. "At least my senior did make the festival more exciting, and for that, I'm genuinely grateful to her. I mean, look at me. Not only did I fail to steal Aigis, but now I don't even know where he is. You'd think someone would notice a walking, talking suit of armor. Maybe I'm the only one to blame if they stop holding my festival. I would be sad, sure, but I guess my senior could throw an even bigger party next year!" She laughed unconvincingly. Her smile was laced with a sadness that made my heart ache.

My chief didn't have a strong endgame, which tended to get her in trouble, but she was also a perfect goddess beloved by all and someone who could get anything done.

She was my ideal woman and a precious friend with whom I could talk about anything, from my improving situations with Megumin and Darkness to my memories of Japan.

And she and I shared secrets, even more than me and Aqua, my fellow migrant from Earth.

She spent all her time doing her goddess work alone in that white room. And when she was a thief, she was by herself, too.

She was my dear friend, my slightly unreliable chief.

And she was the woman I was infatuated with, my hard-working goddess.

"I guess I cause you a lot of trouble, Lowly Assistant. Dragging you off to look for Sacred Treasures or leaving you to keep my senior from going crazy with things." The sweeps of the broom became listless. "I've got to thank you, Lowly Assistant. You're the only one who knows my true identity and about the different things I do. It's not like I'm asking anyone to give me a prize for secretly helping to resist the Demon King's army, but… But thanks to you, I feel like I've gotten a little bit of a reward."

Then the face of the goddess Eris broke into a gentle smile.

……

"Chief…I mean, Lady Eris. I'd like to ask for the cooperation of the people of the Eris Church in something."

Chris looked confused.

I repeated the line I'd delivered to the committee several times already.

"I've got an idea."

3

It was the last day of the festival.

Despite the heat, lots and lots of people attended.

"Hello, dear attendees. It is my pleasure and my honor to have been chosen as MC on this occasion…"

We were at Axel's big public square. Located right in the center of town, it was now home to a stage on which a man in a tuxedo spoke into a magical item that acted like a microphone.

"Welcome to the festival's main event, hosted by the Eris Church! The very first Miss Eris Contest! Let the fun begin!"

A huge cheer went up from the audience gathered in front of the stage.

This was my secret plan to solve everything.

Namely, for the Eris Church to sponsor a Miss Such-and-Such pageant.

"Hey, Lowly Assistant. I really just don't know what to say right now." Chris sounded maybe a touch exasperated.

"Just sit back and enjoy the show, Chief," I said lightly.

I was at least confident that this would liven things up. But at the same time, I was well aware that Eris's often-serious followers might not be thrilled to see their goddess used as an excuse for a beauty pageant.

Right now, though, things were different. If the Eris followers continued to come up short, they might not get another festival to celebrate their beloved goddess. I explained that fact to various Eris followers, starting with Darkness, and ultimately, they went along with my plan.

"I admit, I never expected to have to argue so hard with Darkness," Chris said.

"Just goes to show how much she adores Lady Eris, I guess," I replied.

There had been a lengthy debate with Darkness, in which she said that a beauty contest like this one was blasphemy against Lady Eris, and I countered that it was both to restore the authority of the Eris Church and to help us get the Sacred Treasure back. Eris, I argued, would be willing to wink at a little blasphemy for all that benefit—and somehow, Darkness caved.

Chris fidgeted and scratched her cheek, a little embarrassed. "I don't really care if you use my name, honestly..."

"Well, tell Darkness that. Right up to this morning, she was insisting she wouldn't come here."

Chris and I were in the back, in a place from which we could see the stage and the entire square. We wanted to be in position to catch Aigis the moment he appeared.

Saving the Eris Church wasn't the only reason I had come up with this plan.

The entire contest was bait.

There was a very important Sacred Treasure wandering around town who might leave on some kind of journey at any moment. The quickest way to get that item back would be to get together women who Aigis would be interested in.

And I had requested Darkness to help lay the trap…

"…Hey, do you think the real reason Darkness was so opposed to this contest wasn't the permission at all but—?"

Chris was trying to say something, but I honestly didn't have time for it. I had rented a magical camera just for this day and even made sure to have a telephoto lens available.

I'm sure I don't have to explain why.

I aimed my camera at the stage. It was lined with all the girls in town who were most confident in their looks, all of them wreathed in smiles.

"Well, starting with our first contestant, then… Please tell us your name and age, as well as your job!"

4

I had gotten Chris, Darkness, and the entire Eris Church involved in this gala event, but I had to wonder if Aigis would fall for such an obvious trap.

I was hoping to kill all my birds with one stone, but…

…Dammit, this is really getting to me. I'm sure it'll be fine.

That armor wasn't hard to predict, after all. I hated to admit it, but in some ways, he and I were alike.

I scanned the area, while also stealing glances at the beautiful women who passed one after another across the stage.

Chris had said she thought it was going to be a long day and gone to get something to drink. But I could still see her as I glanced around.

I was sure I would notice a big, shiny suit of armor the moment he appeared.

"Hmm," I muttered, watching one slender beauty. "Personally, she's a bit too thin for my taste, but I do like that face."

<You think so? I think she's the prickly type. But you've got to admire that look. She sure knows how to wear the hell outta that outfit.>

"I admit she looks like a bit of a hen, but I think that's fitting for a thin girl. As far as knowing how to dress, though… Hmm. I really should have included a swimsuit portion in the judging."

<How could you *ever* have left out something so important? What are you, stupid?!>

………

"Gotcha!"

<Whoa! Hey, what are you doing?! This is a big deal; keep out of the way!>

I agreed about the importance of the event, but capturing this guy was sort of the whole point.

I flung the net I'd prepared at Aigis, who had wandered up.

I caught him with his guard down, which meant I also caught him in my net.

"I knew you were stupid enough for this to work! This was all a trap to draw you out!"

<S-say what?! You're sharper than you look, kid. I thought you were just a petty thief, but I guess I was wrong!>

Had Chris and I really had all that trouble catching *this* guy?

I wanted all my effort back.

"Why'd you show up so soon anyway?! The contest hasn't been going for five minutes, and we've already caught you! Apologize to Chris! She went to buy drinks thinking we were going to be here awhile!"

<Uh, d'you think you could keep it down? I can't hear what they're saying about that girl. Listen, the MC is asking her what you have to eat to get a bust that big.>

"…Right, we'll come back to this after we hear the interview. We're gonna stay like this, though, where I have the advantage."

<Yeah, sure. After she leaves the stage, it's on.>

I waited for the moment to come, trying my best not to take my eyes off Aigis. The people around us didn't seem to have paid much attention to the commotion; they were focused on the stage.

At last they finished introducing the girl, and she walked off.

"All right, here we go again! We got in an awful lot of trouble because of you, so come quietly if you know what's good for you!"

<Yeah? Go ahead and try it, kid! They didn't give me an awesome name like Mr. Sacred Armor Aigis for no reason. My master and I cut down a zillion monsters back in the day!>

We were back to yelling at each other, each attempting to seize the initiative, when we heard the MC:

"*Excellent, thank you very much. That was our sweet Sonia! Ah, now there's a bust! But this isn't over! The competition for Best of the Chest isn't settled yet!! Let's have a big round of applause!*"

Aigis and I both looked at the stage even as we clawed at the net.

The next girl to show up was another striking specimen. How striking? She could have held her head high beside Wiz or Darkness…!

<…Hey, you think we could shelve this again until after this girl's turn?>

"…Of course. We'll finish this later."

<'Ppreciate it. Hey, are you sure you don't want to take some photos? Don't worry; I won't run away or anything.>

"………Yeah, I guess you're right. There are all these people here—if a sentient suit of armor were to run away, it would be easy just to ask someone where you went. I won't be able to hold this position forever anyway."

I took my hands off the net and once more pointed my camera toward the stage.

<Hey! Look at that! That's gotta be against the rules! How could you not have required a swimsuit competition?!>

"It wasn't my choice; I had my own problems! My friend said she absolutely wouldn't participate if there was a swimsuit portion! Argh, dammit! I do regret it a little bit; maybe I should have stuck to my guns…"

Aigis and I craned our necks, trying our best to see from the nosebleed seats—

<—Whoa, whoa, whoa! That girl looks really vulnerable like that! I mean, not that I object to a swimsuit in summer!>

"Oh, that's a salesgirl. I had this idea to have all the salesgirls around here dress in swimsuits. We called it an anti-heatstroke measure. And you can splash them with water to cool them off with no problem."

<That's genius. No one can object to an anti-heatstroke measure. You wouldn't want to put the girls in danger. Ooh, I'm not sure about this next one. She's got cute clothes, but the outfit and the makeup are only there to fool you.>

"A natural look is the way to go. Laying on the makeup like that is wrong, wrong, wrong. If I were on the judging panel, I would definitely take off points for too much makeup."

Even as I complained, I clicked the shutter several times.

"Now for our next contestant! You all know her as the Sorry Shopkeeper, the Bride of Bad Luck! Just when her store looked like it would be a success, it turned out to be her imagination! She's here in hopes that the prize money will help her make rent this month! Say hello to the owner of Wiz's Magical Item Shoppe!"

"Yeaaaaah! It's Wiz! Wiz is here! Aww yeah, I always knew Wiz looked best in an apron!"

<Man, I wanna get with a high-level lady like that! She looks so cozy and huggable! I want her inside me! But wizards only like cloth, huh? I guess our callings in life don't match up. Damn! Maybe we could get her to change jobs to something that sees more action on the front lines!!>

Aigis and I were getting awfully excited at Wiz's unexpected appearance. The energy in the crowd was practically electric, and I pitied whoever had to follow Wiz...

"Our next contestants are...oh-ho, some succubus cosplayers! It takes a lot of guts, showing up to an Eris contest dressed like that, but...these... ladies..."

The MC started strong but gradually got quieter and quieter, until he trailed off entirely.

I could see why.

<Whoooooooooooa! What's going on here? Three high-level ladies! The older one to the right and the loli kid on the left, they're great, but—what's with that hottie in the middle?! I've never seen anyone like her! A devil! A devil girl! She's not just devilishly attractive—she's a straight-up devil girl!>

Aigis was so noisy you would think I had smashed him to pieces, but the rest of the crowd had fallen eerily silent.

Three succubi stood on the stage.

In fact, I recognized the ones to the left and right. They were employees of the shop I loved.

The one in the middle, though, the unparalleled beauty—I was a regular, but even I didn't recognize her.

I was going to have to ask for her services the next time I was in.

The succubus in the middle plucked the microphone from the hand of the frozen MC.

"*Well, everyone,*" she said, "*you must be getting bored with these contestants... As your scandalous new host, I'll be getting rid of the last few shreds of these skimpy clothes and ushering you all into a world of sensual delight...!*"

Her voice was so alluring that just listening to it sent chills down my spine. And then she put a hand to her clothing.

Succubus costumes were already sexy enough, but now every single eye in the square was focused on her.

No one made so much as a peep but only swallowed heavily and watched, clinging to a fervent hope.

Was she really going to take it off in front of this entire crowd?!

Was she serious?!

Had the buzz of the festival caught up with these erotic monsters? Were they going to show us their true forms?!

<C-camera! Get the camera! Come on—pay attention!>

"Oh crap, yeah! That was a close one…! I guess that's an experienced succubus for you; she sure knows how to please!"

As I got the camera ready to take the shot of my life, the beauty in front of us moved to take off her clothing…!

"And I shed beautifully! Bwa-ha-ha-ha-ha, did you take me for a passing succubus queen? Sorry! It was me, the part-timer at Wiz's Magical Item Shoppe, all along! Ah, the animosity of an entire public square full of people is an exquisite and unique flavor! I'm also currently offering consultations at Wiz's Magical Item Shoppe! If you have any troubles, I'll be there to lend an ear!"

．．．．．．．．

"Please don't throw things! I understand your feelings, honored audience, but please don't throw things at me!"

Vanir and the two succubi walked away, leaving the MC to suffer the hail of garbage flung by the crowd.

Some of it contributed by Aigis and myself, naturally.

When the commotion finally died down, the MC collected himself and made a broad gesture toward the edge of the stage.

"O-okay, our next contestant is one of our top candidates today. I don't think there's a soul in this town who doesn't know her! Part adventurer, part reigning queen of the Endurance Championship. And now…here to participate in the Miss Eris Contest, scion of the noble Dustiness family, Lady Lalatina Ford Dustiness!"

Yesss! Now we're talking!

Although it was pretty much irrelevant, since Aigis was already here, I had asked Darkness, who ranked highly in the looks department if nothing else, to be our bait for the armor. I had hoped to ask Megumin, too, but sadly, she was still in prison.

When Darkness showed up, Aigis went wild. <Whoo! Yes, yes, a thousand times yes! Pretty face, *great* body, and a noble?! Sign me up!>

Darkness, maybe with an eye toward the contest, had dressed like a noblewoman going out while trying to beat the heat. She had on the pure-white dress she sometimes wore around the house, but she was also wearing a touch of makeup, and she had braided her hair, then topped it all off with a wide-brimmed hat.

She was looking at the ground, using the hat to hide her face, which had turned red with all the attention from the crowd.

"You'd better believe it, buddy. That's my party member. I told her we would need some serious bait to catch you, and that's how I got her to be a part of this."

<Seriously?! Aww, man, you're so lucky! Hey, I want her to be my master! I swear, nary a scratch would sully that hot, hot bod!>

Heck, not only had I caught him, I'd brought him around.

"But she's a Crusader, you know? Ever present on the front lines, her whole job is to soak up enemy attacks. Weren't you saying that even armor feels pain? Plus, maybe you can't tell because she's wearing clothes, but that girl is *ripped*."

<Is she? Well, but that's… But a Crusader… Shoot! Why'd she have to be a Crusader…? Man, but she's *really* my type in the looks department. I wonder if there's a chance anyone better will come along…?>

I sympathized with Aigis's disappointment. True, in looks, at least—face and overall sexiness—Darkness was a ten out of ten.

If only she'd had a personality to match. She was a surprising amount of trouble.

What a waste…

"Let's keep watching; there are other contestants still."

<Yeah, no need to jump to any conclusions before I've seen everyone. Ooh, the interview is starting!>

"Now, then! I think most people here are familiar with you, but kindly tell us your name, age, and job!"

"...I'm Lalatina Ford Dustiness... I'm eighteen years old, and I'm currently acting governor..."

Darkness must have been really nervous, because her voice was practically a whisper even through the microphone. I was pretty far away, and I could still tell how tense she looked.

It was then that one of the adventurers in the crowd shouted: "Lalatiiina! Speak up so we can heeear youuu!"

This inspired several more hecklers.

"Young Lady, you look lovely as ever today!"

"What happened to your armor? Not that you don't look wonderful like that, Lalatina!"

I wasn't the only one who had a reputation around these parts; Darkness had become pretty well-known, too. A few drunken adventurers who recognized her had decided to poke some fun.

Seeing Darkness blushing bright red and ready to cry, I couldn't resist the urge to torment her a little bit.

"Way to go, Lalatina!" I cried. "How about you show us those famous abs of yours?!"

<I thought you said she was your party member?>

"And you think that means I ought to encourage her or something, dumbass? Look at her glare at the audience, all blushy and teary. You ever seen someone look that excited? She's gonna win for sure."

<I get it. You sure know how to play the game. All right, I'll help you! Nice work, lady; show us some skin!>

Now Aigis got in on the act, and it fanned the flames among the other adventurers.

"He's right, just a bit!"

"Don't you have a swimsuit or something?!"

"Lift up your skirt, milady!"

The shouts from the audience were escalating quickly. Darkness, normally useless, was getting the same level of attention as a Japanese pop idol. I was thrilled about that, so I shouted as loudly as I could: "Take it ooofffff!"

That caused Darkness to immediately fix me with a death stare.

Whoops. She found me.

"Yeah, take it off!"

"Do it, Darkness!"

"Strip! Tease! Strip! Tease!"

<Strip! Tease! Strip! Tease!>

At that moment, the entire square was united with one heart, and everyone raised their voices in a single beautiful chant...!

"And just what are you up to?"

The chill in Chris's voice was like ice-cold water raining down on Aigis and me.

5

"Argh, I can't believe you two. Bullying my friend like that."

"You've got it all wrong—when I saw Darkness getting that big cheer, I just wanted to give her a boost, like a top idol..."

"A top idol who was being bullied into doing a striptease? ... And, Aigis, look at you... You're supposed to be one of the best Sacred Treasures..."

Somewhere out beyond the back of the crowd, Aigis and I were bowing repeatedly to Chris, who was looking pitiful with tears in her eyes.

I finally gave a deep sigh and said to her, "But hey, at least we captured this guy, like we planned all along. And the Eris Church got a big, popular event going. All good, right?"

"It's nowhere near good! Just look at this!"

The audience seating area was currently filled with shouting and arguing.

Darkness, finally broken by the calls to strip, had jumped into the audience and begun attacking adventurers. They fought back as hard as they could, but in a fistfight, Darkness had the overwhelming advantage.

...Actually, maybe I should have been sending her into battle with monsters barehanded.

<This has gotten fun. That's one strong lady! Beautiful women and fistfights are the flowers of any festival. I can feel the blood dancing in my veins! Burn hot, my passion! Shine bright, my body! Okay, I'm getting in there!>

"Please stay out of any more trouble! Aww, Aigis, please—I need at least *one* of you to act like an adult... When the Demon King is safely defeated, I'll use my authority as goddess to grant the wish not just of the hero who defeated him but yours as well..."

Chris put a hand to her forehead, letting out a breath at the sight of Aigis, who was all excited about jumping into the fray.

Aigis only shrugged. <Is she still talking about being a goddess? Listen to me, sweetheart. I know goddesses. I mean literally, I've met one. In fact, it was a goddess who gave me to a certain young woman. So I can tell you firsthand: Goddesses are bad news.>

"Say *what*?!"

He wasn't wrong. In my mind, I pictured the person who had probably sent him here, who at that very moment was busy being bad news with her precious church.

"You! *You!!* Oh, now I'm angry! I'm going to seal you at the bottom of a lake until I find an owner for you! Lucky for you, it's the same place I've put the other Sacred Treasures, so you can get to know them while you wait!"

<A punch like that might as well be sticks and stones, sweetheart! I'm a Sacred Treasure, remember? Ha, but feel free to give it another shot, missy!>

"Hrrrgh!"

Chris launched another painful-looking punch at Aigis; I took a quick glance around. Everyone else was still busy watching Darkness tear up the spectator seating. Admittedly, this wasn't what I had been expecting when I planned this event, but it was definitely exciting.

What about our original objectives, though?

Chris's and my goal had been to draw out Aigis.

The other idea, however, had been to help the Eris Church claw back some of their clout in the festival, and as far as that went...

...we had, regrettably, made zero progress toward that goal.

"Ah, it's good to laugh. What else was going to happen with a beauty contest here? All the gorgeous women in this town have something wrong with them. Anyone could have seen this coming. Given it was run by that uptight Eris Church, it turned out to be some good fun, don't you think?"

The voice was that of an audience member in front of us.

"Yes, well, I suppose so. But I'm thinking maybe the Axis Church can handle this festival alone next year. They may all be morons, but they sure know how to throw a party."

"You've got that right—fools and idiots, every one of 'em, but they're always a good time! Stupid, though!"

Other voices chimed in nearby, and several audience members seemed ready to go home. Maybe they felt they had seen most of the good-looking girls in town by this point.

Chris stopped pounding on Aigis.

"I know how hard the Eris Church works, but if we're only going to have one festival a year, I think it's better to make it a flashy one."

"You're absolutely right. Did you know they're arguing that it should be just the Aqua Appreciation Festival starting next year? They've even got a petition going."

"Huh! It sounds like there's even more stupidity going on at the Axis booths today. Looks like things are over here; want to go check it out?"

And then...

"Ah... Ah-ha-ha. My children try so hard, but it looks like it's game over. I guess we really will lose the festival next year." Despite how obviously sad she was, Chris tried to smile, as if to spare me from worrying about her. "It's just as well. I never *really* had time to enjoy this festival. While we're here celebrating, there are people being tormented by monsters... And that's why I need every Sacred Treasure I can get my hands on."

And then Chris, who had done everything to this point as quietly as she could so as not to be noticed by anyone, turned to face Aigis. She was acting as casual as anything.

"Come on, Aigis, please? Won't you go along with me?"

<Uh... I'm touched, really, but don't expect me to go along with you just because you made some puppy-dog eyes at me!>

....

"Hey, Aigis," I offered. "If I were to introduce you to a super-gorgeous woman, would you do what Chris asked?"

He replied, <Huh? Super-gorgeous...? Hey, you think I can't see through you? You're talking about that masked guy from earlier! You're going to get him to change into a beautiful woman and then try to foist him off on me! Well, canny old Aigis won't fall for—>

I ignored the chatty armor, turning to look at Chris and bowing my head. "Chief. Er, no—let me call you Lady Eris just this once. I've got a little...okay, a really big favor to ask."

Chris quailed at my gesture of respect, but...

<Wha—? I thought her name was Chris. What are you doing, calling her Lady Eris? Don't tell me you're one of these crazy— Ha-haaa, touch of heatstroke? Has the temperature gotten to you? And here you were the one bragging about anti-heatstroke measures. I do need to thank you for giving me something nice to look at. I'll go get a doctor—>

"It's all right, Lowly Assistant... I mean, Kazuma. I will hear you.

If it's within my power, simply ask." And then Chris looked me right in the eye.

<Hey, hey! I'm gonna get a little annoyed if you keep ignoring me, all right? Hey, what are you planning?> Aigis was making unhappy sounds of metal on metal.

"Pay attention, Aigis," I said. "I've got a girl you're gonna *worship*."

6

Event staff finally corralled the raging Darkness, took her to another area, and calmed her down.

There was still some chattering, but things had finally gotten quiet enough to proceed. Onstage, the MC took the mic in hand once more.

"Now, then. It looks like things have quieted down a bit, and we have no more contestants. That means it's time to announce the victor of the Miss Eris—"

But that was as far as he got.

The noise in the square stopped instantaneously.

The shouting adventurers.

The merchants who had been getting ready to leave.

Every single person around.

Everyone there from every walk of life was focused completely and exclusively on the stage.

No one knew when the girl standing before them had gotten there, but she wore a gentle smile.

"...Uh... Huh? Um..." As everyone stared at the girl, the MC tried to muster something to say. *".........Um. It appears we have...a walk-on contestant...and that's...just fine, I think...?"*

The girl stood on the stage, still smiling quietly.

That's right.

*   *   *

Her face, her clothes, everything about her would have been immediately familiar to anyone from this world: She was the spitting image of the goddess Eris.

"You're right. I'm sorry for just jumping in," Eris said, placing her hands together. She bowed her head. It was enough to set the MC reeling.

"N-n-n-n-n-not at all! Not in the least! Don't you worry about it! Th-thank you very much for participating in today's Miss Lady Eris Contest!"

The fact that it had suddenly become the Miss *Lady* Eris Contest implied that the MC had realized, however dimly, who was standing in front of him.

But not everyone, it seemed, had overcome their feelings of disbelief. Time seemed to start moving in the square again, a murmur—but not a very loud one—spreading through the crowd. Beside me, Aigis didn't make a peep.

Finally, the MC seemed to collect himself, and he held out the mic for Eris with a certain reluctance.

"A-all right, then... Please forgive me for asking the same thing we ask all our contestants, but...if possible, perhaps you could tell us your name...?"

He sounded fearful and somehow hopeful at the same time. Eris smiled at the crowd in a way that caused everyone present to draw a collective breath.

"My name is Eris."

The moment she spoke, a cheer rocked the square. A frenzied shouting of Eris's name.

Some people were just gazing up at her, as if they had fallen in love. Others had placed their hands together in prayer. Some of the people

around us, presumably Eris followers, were weeping and prostrating themselves.

"M-man, so this is the power of a real goddess. This is a bigger reaction than even I expected, gosh."

A little bit overwhelmed by the shouting, I turned to Aigis, who had been standing stock-still beside me. Now, though, he started to shiver.

<I've found her...,> he whispered. <I've found her. I've found heeerrrrrr! Yes, that's her! That's my master if anyone! Is this real life?! Seriously, what's going on?! How can a woman that gorgeous even exist in this world?! It doesn't make any sense! It just doesn't make any sense to me!!>

"H-hey, calm down! I didn't think suits of armor were even supposed to have personalities, and yours is the worst!"

As I worked to talk down Aigis, onstage, the MC was trying his best to ask another question.

"Ahhh, yes-yes-yes, th-thank you very much! Thank you so much for your most gracious answer! Uh, normally there would be two further questions…" The MC looked thrilled but sounded very intimidated.

Those other two questions were the ones about her age and job.

Eris giggled and said, "Those answers are secret." Then she gave a mischievous wink and held up her pointer finger in a hush-hush gesture.

There was another bout of raucous cheering, until the air itself started to shake.

There was someone else—or should I say some*thing* else—here that was acting kind of weird. The self-proclaimed Sacred Treasure shouted out, <N-no, stop! Lady Eris, there's no need for any more fan service! I, Aigis, will not let you strike such a devilish pose!>

"You're the one who needs to stop. It's like I don't even know who you are anymore! One thing you are is awfully noisy, though, so pipe down. I'll introduce you to her later!"

<You will?! Really?! A punk like you... I mean, a fine gentleman like yourself can introduce me to her?!>

"Damn right I can. Didn't I tell you? I said I would introduce you to a gorgeous woman if you did what Chris said. Incidentally, that *is* Chris there, as well as the goddess Eris. She told you over and over who she was, but you didn't even listen."

<Fuuuck! Damn it all, wh-what am I gonna do? How can I apologize to Lady Eris?! H-hey, I'll let you inside me for an hour if you just help me apologize to her!>

Frankly, I had zero interest in being inside Aigis, but I thought maybe if I helped him out here, he would finally listen to Eris.

From the stage, Eris looked directly at Aigis and me and giggled again.

"The goddess Lady Eris has descended to walk among uuusssss!" somebody shouted. I gave her a wry smile back.

"Lady Eris, please, please shake my hand! I've been so unlucky recently—please give me the blessing of the goddess of good fortune!"

I couldn't tell who had spoken. It might have been a testament to the sincerity of the prayer that it was audible over the hum and roar of the crowd.

The cry seemed to cause the entire place to fall silent.

...*Huh? Wait, this doesn't seem right.*

"Me too! Lady Eris, take my hand!"

"Me first, idiot!"

"Lady Eris, there's a hungry cat waiting for me at home. Please help me win the lottery on my way back...!"

Impassioned audience members started trying to climb up onto the stage.

"*Please stay calm, everyone!*" the MC said. "*Please stay off the stage!*" But the announcer's cries did nothing to stop the crowd.

Onstage, Eris looked lost and concerned, but nonetheless she reached out delicately to take the hand outstretched to her.

Why would you let yourself get pushed around so easily, Lady Eris? You could just turn the guy down.

Nearby, I heard two Eris followers shouting to each other before they rushed off.

"Hey, we've got to protect Lady Eris!"

"Y-yeah, we can't let this go on! Look, they're getting so carried away that they won't let go of her hand!"

I agreed with them: I didn't like the way this was going. It was like an idol meet-and-greet gone bad; it was only a matter of time until somebody did something truly heinous.

"Help me out here, Aigis! Lady Eris is gonna get hurt at this rate! If you really want to show her you're sorry, then use yourself to protect her!"

<Yeah! Who could have predicted a twist so favorable to a suit of armor?! I'll protect her—I'll super-protect her! I, the sacred armor Aigis, shall protect the chaste jewel that is Lady Eris to my dying breath!>

"Ch-chaste? I don't think you... Actually, since she doesn't seem to know anything about love, maybe she is..."

<Lady Eris is a goddess! She must be a virgin! I'm sure she's the kind of girl who, if she were faced with the grimy naked body of a man, would cry out and cover her face. But then she would peek through her fingers, because she would be just the slightest bit interested by the sight. She's gentle and kindhearted, and I'm sure she smells wonderful.>

Man, he was really smitten.

"Come on—let's hurry! When we get up onstage, you surround Lady Eris! Then we bust through the crowd!"

<Awesome! I never dreamed I would get to be one with Lady Eris so soon! L-Lady Eris...inside me... *Pant, pant...*>

"You're starting to sound like the most dangerous guy of all; is this really a good idea?! Anyway, take care of the crowd in front of us—you're a walking weapon, aren't you?!"

Aigis responded by shoving his way through the crowd.

<Damn right I am! And now that I've found my true master, I'm hotter than anyone in this square! You there, outta my way! I'm so superheated I'll burn anyone who touches me!>

"Errrgyahhh! Who is this guy? Who would be stupid enough to wear armor that hot?!"

"Hey, don't push. I don't care how hot you— No, sto— Aggghhh!"

"Somebody dump some water on this guy! Water!"

I understood. Aigis had been out in the sun for so long that now he was burning hot. He worked his way through the crowd as various audience members fled from him, while I got to the stage as fast as I could.

Eris was still politely clasping hands with people. "K-Kazuma!" she said, looking worried. "What do we do? This is getting messy…"

"Aigis is on his way here. I want you to get inside him and go somewhere deserted! …Hey, you, give Lady Eris her hand back! If you wanna hold on to someone for so long, I'll give you my hand instead!"

"Ahhh, stop! I was never going to wash this hand again!"

I was forcibly exchanging pulling Eris's hand from the grasp of one of the audience members and replacing it with mine when Aigis dragged himself out of the crowd and up onto the stage.

<Sorry to keep you waiting, Master. Please get inside me, quickly! The magic phrase to unlock me is 'I'm gonna be ol' Aigis's bride!' Go for it!>

"I-I'm gonna be ol' Aigis's—"

"Please don't let him trick you, Lady Eris. And as for you, we don't have time for games!"

Aigis gave a disappointed shrug. <Aww, too bad… Oh well, here we go, Master! *Com-bine*!>

There was a bright flash. The intensity of it caused everyone nearby, including the MC, the entire audience, and me to shield our eyes. Then we finally looked back at Eris…!

Ensconced in the armor, the goddess began squealing. "Ahhh, it's hot! Kazuma, it's hot; I'm going to fry in here!"

Crap! That's right—Aigis was really warm just then!

I raised my right hand and pointed it at the armor.

"*Freeze!!*"

[But the spell has no effect.]

Argh, that's right—spells and skills didn't work on this guy!

"Is Lady Eris gone?!"

"Where'd she go?!"

"Could she have gone back to her heavenly home?"

"No, those two guys who climbed up on the stage did something!"

It appeared to the audience that Eris had vanished in that flash of light, and now they began to mount the stage, pointing at Aigis and me.

"I don't like where this is going... Hey, Aigis! I'll distract them and try to hold them off for a while. You take Lady Eris and run!"

<Leave it to me! And here's a special tip for all your hard work: Lady Eris really does smell wonderful!>

This guy is hopeless.

Not that I wasn't slightly happy to receive that information!

"K-Kazuma?! Those people look murderous; you're going to be in danger...!" Eris said, her voice muffled by the armor. Maybe she didn't have time to be concerned about Aigis's impropriety.

I tried to reassure her as best I could.

"It's all right. They're all barehanded. The way I'm feeling now, none of them can beat me."

If they didn't have any weapons, then with my Drain Touch skill, I held the advantage.

I turned to the crowd trying to get up onto the stage and said, "This ought to cool you off! *Create Water!*"

The moment I shouted, a veritable flood crashed down on their heads!

"Glurg?! That son of a—!"

"Aww, now he's done it! Come here, you!"

"That's the Adventurer Kazuma—he's famous for how weak he is! Let's get him!"

Now they were sopping wet *and* ready to kill me. At least I had gotten their attention.

Maybe Eris was resisting Aigis, though, because the armor made no move to escape.

"Go, Chief," I said. "It's the duty of a lackey to sacrifice himself when his leader is going to be captured."

"L-Lowly Assistant…"

I turned my back on Aigis, who still hadn't moved.

"Plus, today is the last day of the festival!" I added. "And festivals mean two things: shop stalls and fireworks. And they say fighting is the flower of a festival!" I put up my dukes. "Come and get meeeeee!!"

"Lowly Assistant!"

Maybe Aigis finally got a move on, because Eris's voice seemed to be getting farther away as I launched myself at the crowd…!

7

Darkness stood with her arms crossed, glaring down at me.

"Well, Mr. Kingpin, what do you have to say for yourself?"

After getting into a gigantic fistfight at the beauty contest, I had been taken in by the police and tossed into a holding cell. They told me to just cool my head for a bit and then left me there to sit sadly with my knees drawn up into my chest, even though it was the last day of the festival…

"Look. I'm grateful to you for rescuing me and all, but what's the big idea?"

I had been set free thanks to Darkness's intercession, but no sooner had I gotten home than she made me kneel formally in the living room.

Beside me was Aqua, also sitting on her knees, with Emperor Zel in her arms and a sparkle in her eyes.

Apparently, she had something to answer for, too. The at-least-I'm-not-the-only-one-getting-in-trouble look on her face kind of bugged me, though.

Megumin, who had also been released after Darkness talked to the police, was leaning on the sofa, watching me with a look of exasperation.

"And what do you mean, *kingpin?*" I said. "Tell me exactly what happened while I was in police custody."

I couldn't think of anything I'd done to feel guilty about, but nonetheless, I kept my hands in front of me on the carpet so that I could throw myself into a posture of abject apology if the discussion turned sour.

"First, let me ask you something... When you spoke to the merchants' council, did you really tell them that pitting the Axis and Eris Churches against each other would be the best way to boost profits?"

Without missing a beat, I lowered myself into a perfect formal bow of apology.

Darkness didn't even hesitate but kept talking. "And according to Aqua, the person who first thought of cosponsoring the Eris Appreciation Festival wasn't her but you. And according to the council president, lewd ideas like putting the salesgirls in swimsuits and having a costume parade were yours, too... Here, 'Honored Adviser.' Have a look at this. The president brought it to me by way of apology."

Apparently, she had found everything out when the council president had come here personally to apologize. Now that I thought about it, I realized he probably had no idea Darkness and I lived in the same house.

What was I gonna do? The collective gaze in the room on me was so cold. Maybe if I pretended I'd gone into shock, they'd let it go.

"Don't look so pitiful, Kazuma. You'll make us feel like *we're* the ones bullying *you*," Darkness said. "In any event, the practice of skimming some of the profits from the festival is an ugly relic left behind by the former governor. It's not your fault—you can accept this proudly… Come on, Honored Adviser; do you really not want it?"

Darkness pretended to look concerned as she held out the bulging sack of money.

Stop—please stop. It would be better if you yelled your lungs out at me.

"Well, hold on, Darkness. There's something else that bothers me more than this," Megumin said, preparing to lob another bomb my way. "Kazuma. I hear tell that you are on good terms with a number of women these days. For example, I hear that you were up drinking until dawn with a certain succubus cosplayer lady. I am not saying you were wrong to do it. It's not like you're dating anyone, after all."

"Y-you really lived it up, didn't you…?" Darkness said. "I mean, we don't really have the kind of relationship where I can criticize you for it, but after you and I got so far along, do you really think that's appropriate?"

Aww, not Darkness, too.

Megumin did a double take when she heard this.

"I think I just heard something I cannot ignore! When exactly did you 'get so far along'? How far along did you get? What base carnality, to get so carried away by the festival that you jump straight to having physical relations!"

"W-wait, what…?!" Darkness exclaimed. "W-we haven't had physical relations yet…!"

"Did you say 'yet'? Meaning that one day you expect to have them, you despicable cur!"

I turned my attention away from the sudden catfight.

"Hey, Aqua, do you think I'm sort of like the star of a harem thing right now?"

"You look awfully happy for someone who's being forced to sit and apologize in his own living room."

Whether because she had overheard us or just to keep Megumin from attacking her any more, Darkness said, "Th-that's right, Aqua! You're next! Just what do you intend to do about everything that's happened?" Darkness's hair was disheveled, and she sounded a bit panicked.

"...Come on, Darkness; let's talk about this. Even that masked demon said it. Humans are a race that has conversations."

Come to think of it, I still didn't know what she had actually done.

"That's true—you're right. I do believe talking to one another is important. If we had started with a conversation, things might never have gotten so out of hand."

Aqua sat beside me, still with her knees tucked under her and still with Emperor Zel in her arms. She was making one of her rare logical pronouncements, and Darkness slowed down to answer.

I finally got to hear the whole story.

It was the day of the Eris beauty contest.

The Axis disciples, flush with their recent run of sales, were intent on striking the final blow to the Eris Church, which they planned to do with an idea Aqua had come up with. That would be the secret plan Cecily had talked about.

Aqua, who was a total idiot except when it came to Japanese street stalls, apparently, had hit upon a brilliant, awful idea.

"I can't believe you actually came up with a plan like this," Megumin said, sounding really impressed. "It certainly would result in a lot of money for the person who started it. It's almost too good an idea to believe it's really yours, Aqua."

Darkness leaned in, unmoved. "And who taught you about this 'pyramid scheme'? You didn't come up with such a high-level crime on your own, did you?" She brought her face right up to Aqua's.

Aqua looked away and pointed directly at...

...me.

"Hey, don't try to pin this on me! Yeah, I admit that one time, way back when we were still mired in debt, I complained that I had no hope of paying the money back and wondered aloud if I should start a pyramid scheme or something! And yeah, I admit that I explained how they work!"

"So it *was* you! How much trouble do you have to cause here before you'll be satisfied?"

"Hey, this was *not* my idea! It's a well-known crime in my country, and... Hey, Aqua, you knew full well it was illegal, didn't you?! Don't you pretend you can't hear me!"

That's right: This idiot had deployed her followers in the service of a pyramid scheme. Apparently, she figured that in a world with less elaborate laws than Earth's, she was entitled to whatever she could get away with. Given the huge crowd present for the festival, her system spread instantly and made a staggering amount of money in just one day.

Too much money.

Enough money that Darkness found out about it.

Aqua, who had been listening politely until that moment, suddenly faced Darkness head-on and exclaimed, "I didn't have any choice! The Eris Church had that juvenile Miss Whatever Contest, and they were going to outperform us! Plus, it's going to take a lot of money if we want to host the Aqua Appreciation Festival by ourselves next year, so—!"

"And you think that's an excuse to commit a crime?! This all started because you demanded to be included in the festival..."

"Aww, but it's not *fair* for the festival to be all about Eris! Why don't *I* have a festival? Why doesn't anyone venerate *me*? I want to be worshipped and pampered! Anyway, a pyramid scheme isn't a crime yet!"

"That's true for now. *For now!* That just means it's a new form of fraud that we haven't yet made laws against, but it's still outrageous behavior!"

As the temperature rose between them, Megumin and I looked at each other and smiled.

"If the law hasn't caught up with me, then nothing about my idea was illegal! So give me back the money I made! Give me back the money for next year's Aqua Appreciation Festival!!"

"That money has already been returned to your victims! If you push any harder, you're going to find yourself with a criminal record like Megumin and Kazuma!"

"P-pardon me, but I was merely put in jail and told to cool down. I do not have a criminal record!"

"Y-yeah, and I got off with a warning!"

The sun had well and truly set when I arrived at a party venue in the downtown district.

"You're late, Kazuma; we've all gotten started already! Come on over here!"

I guess it wasn't quite what you'd call an after-party. More of a shindig to close out the event on the last night of the festival.

The party venue they had rented out was now filled with people who had been a part of the recently concluded festival. That meant everyone from councillors and staff to members of the Eris and Axis Churches.

I found a seat next to Aqua. "Hey, isn't having you and them in the same room like having a goddess and a devil in a cage together?"

Aqua grimaced at my simile. "Listen, Kingpin NEET, I think it's going overboard to compare the children of the Eris Church to devils. And we're celebrating the end of the festival here, aren't we? My children always make it a point not to fight at a party."

Actually, I had been thinking of the *Axis* Church people as the devils, but whatever.

Plus, just like Aqua said, the Axis followers in the room weren't

harassing the Eris people—in fact, they were pouring drinks and generally having a good time.

"Is there any chance you guys would always be this nice if we just let you party all the time?"

"I can't shake the sense that you're making fun of me, but you're not wrong. By the way, for your reference, the same is true of me. If you want me to behave, just bring me expensive wine every day."

"So you finally admit you're the cause of half my problems around here."

I recognized various people around the party hall. There was the priestess Cecily, rubbing her drunken-red cheek up against a girl from the Eris Church; there was Wiz drinking and eating with Vanir (why? Had he been part of the staff downtown?), who had brought Yunyun along.

And...

"Come on, Darkness—drink up! You too, Megumin!"

"Why do you always get so excitable when there's wine involved? D-don't try to get Megumin to drink! Here, I'll take her share!"

"Darkness, I am no longer a child, so please let me enjoy this moment with a little alcohol! I'm even old enough to get married! Oh, Kazuma, you're late. You tell her, Kazuma! I'm just two years younger than you, so we're practically the same age!"

And there was Chris, her face red, sitting with Darkness and Megumin.

Did all goddesses love parties?

"It's way too soon for you to start drinking," I said. "And the difference in our ages is back to three years, because guess what? Today is my birthday!"

That's right: Today marked one year since I had come to this world.

I knew it was kind of sad to announce your own birthday, but frankly, I wanted everyone to celebrate me.

I turned to Aqua expectantly.

"Hmm. Congrats, I guess? So, Kazuma, where's my present?"

Ah, sweet words of celebration…

"…*Your* present? What are you talking about? Why would I give you a present?"

"Oh, that's right, Kazuma. I forgot you're a big dummy who doesn't know anything about this country's customs. Well, let me enlighten you. Around here, on their birthday, a person is so grateful to everyone around them for helping them survive another year that they give presents to all their friends."

No way. Stupid, rotten country.

Then again, in a world full of monsters out to shorten the average life span, I guess it made a certain kind of sense…

"There is no such custom," Megumin broke in. "Happy birthday, Kazuma. When we get home, I'll give you something wonderful."

No sooner had Megumin spoken than I tore into Aqua. "Why, you, telling believable lies, you're just an old hag of indeterminate age whose birthday we don't even know! How about you tell me *your* birthday and how old you are!"

"Waaaaahhh! Kazuma said the unforgivable—again! I really will punish you this time!"

As Aqua and I chewed each other out, Darkness, who was using a handkerchief to hold her glass, said, "Kazuma, happy birthday. I'll also give you some kind of present when we get home. I'm sorry—if I'd known, I could have had something for you already."

"Awesome, thanks. You're right; maybe I should've said something earlier. Megumin had her birthday without me even knowing it, and I'd like to celebrate the next one properly. For that matter, Darkness, when's your birthday? I know you're a noble, even if you're not much of one—I'll bet you throw a wicked party."

Darkness suddenly started acting a little funny. "Uh… M-my birthday? …Well, that's, it's, uh…"

As Darkness sat there with her eyes brimming, Chris said nonchalantly, "Darkness's birthday is way over, I think. Didn't you have some huge party back around spring? Say, Lowly Assistant, why didn't you and your friends come?"

Darkness twitched, and everything fell into place for me.

"You deliberately didn't invite us to your party because you were afraid we would cause trouble! You thought we would do something to the other nobles!"

"Is that true?!" Aqua exclaimed. "That's terrible! Come to think of it, Darkness, you wanted us to leave before that Iris girl could give us our awards, too!"

"Let's give her what's coming to her!" Megumin said. "Let this misunderstanding young noble receive her comeuppance!"

Darkness was practically in tears under this concerted assault. Chris was watching the whole thing with a bit of a smirk; then she tugged on my sleeve as if to suggest we take a walk.

"That sure got out of control fast… Ugh, I heard from Darkness, okay? She said you were the ringleader in all this."

The words came suddenly, and a little bit sullenly, from Chris as we were walking around outside the party venue, me enjoying the cool night breeze against my wine-warmed face.

This was after I'd had Eris herself appear in her own beauty pageant.

I guess having a goddess show up was a pretty big deal, and people had used magic and messenger birds and post horses, every method available, to let the surrounding towns and even the capital know what had happened.

According to the council members, it was likely that from now on, Axel, the town where the goddess appeared, would be treated as a holy place by the Eris Church.

"Y-yeah, I'm really sorry about that. I'll keep helping you with your Sacred Treasure search, so please forgive me… But the councillors told me something. They said that after this, the Eris Appreciation Festival *has* to go on, no matter what."

Chris looked pleased about that. "Oh yeah...? Then between that and the way you and Aigis rescued me on that stage, I guess I can forgive you!"

"Oh, thank you, Goddess!"

As we bantered back and forth, we wandered through a town still enjoying the last embers of excitement from the festival.

I gathered that after Aigis safely escaped the beauty contest, he had started to listen to Chris. They would soon be trying to find him a master, someone to whom they could give him as a trump card against the Demon King's army. Aigis hoped for a Sword Master, and Chris hoped to grant his wish as best she could.

And so it seemed like both our latest Sacred Treasure search and the little Eris-versus-Axis showdown had turned out okay.

When I reviewed everything in my mind, though, I couldn't help being struck by how much influence a real goddess could have. I mean, we were just walking around, and...

"*Sigh...* I wonder if she could still be somewhere in town—Lady Eris. I've adored her ever since I first saw her picture..."

"Even if she were still here, she would never show herself to a black-hearted sinner like you. She would pick a devout, pure follower like me."

"Oh, you're not so great. You used a teleport service to get here as fast as you could after you stole your girlfriend's dowry."

"Jerk, I came to get Lady Eris's blessing on my marriage—my girl even said it was okay, you hear me?"

Just a couple of guys talking on the street, and they were talking about Eris.

As we passed by, I said, "...You heard 'em, Lady Eris. It's probably fine if you don't bless them, right?"

"I'm not Lady Eris; I'm Lady Chris, Lowly Assistant. All I could do right now is swipe some treasure from your house to pay back the dowry that guy took."

Then both of us broke into laughter.

Maybe it was the stopping and laughing that caused the people behind Chris to suddenly run into her.

The culprits were a pair of small sisters, each carrying a lovely flower.

"S-sorry!" one of them said.

"We're very sorry!" added the other quickly.

Chris replied, "I'm the one who should apologize, just stopping suddenly like that! Are you both okay? You didn't fall down, did you?" She bowed her head again.

The flower belonging to the girl who looked like the younger sister had fallen to the ground. Chris hurriedly picked it up.

"Gee, I'm sorry! I made you drop your chris!" Then she picked up the purple flower and handed it to the girl.

"Chris?" I whispered, eyeing the bloom. "...Is that the name of that flower?"

"Sure it is. This kind of flower is called a chris. In the language of flowers, it represents the resolve to never give up."

The girl who appeared to be the older of the two made a sound of admiration. "Wow. Hey, why do you have a scar on your cheek? Does that mean you're an adventurer? My daddy said adventurers are all ruffians, but then how do you know about flowers?"

Out of the mouths of babes: Chris was at a loss. She scratched her scar shyly. "Um... This scar, I got it while fighting the bad guys, the Demon King's army. And yes, I'm an adventurer, but there are some of us who are decent people. Like this guy here." She looked at me and giggled. "And that flower's the only one I know anything about. See how it's the same color as my eyes? I adore the chris flower."

She leaned over and looked at the girls, then brought the flower up to her face to smell the aroma.

"Wow, that's neat. We're gonna offer these flowers to Lady Eris. Big Sis and I used our allowance to buy them."

"Yeah, they say Lady Eris likes this flower, too!"

"Huh! I'm impressed with you, knowing what Lady Eris likes! But I think if Lady Eris knew that little girls like you were using their precious allowance to bring her an offering—well, she'd certainly be happy, but she'd be a little concerned, too. So I think she'd be perfectly pleased if this was the only offering you two brought her."

"Really...? But we wanted to thank Lady Eris."

"Thank her...?" Chris looked puzzled.

"Yeah, that's right. Our mommy said that the reason everyone can live in peace here is because Lady Eris bestows powers on people to resist the evil Demon King."

"And she said Lady Eris works hard, but nobody knows about it. So we wanted to say thanks to her and try to encourage her."

Hearing that, Chris said, "I-is that right...? Well, from now on, I think Lady Eris would be very happy just to know how you feel, even without any offerings. I'm sure she would thank *you* for encouraging her." She still seemed like she wasn't completely sure what to say. But she scratched her cheek again with an expression that was both embarrassed and deeply relieved.

The younger girl looked at her and said, "...Come to think of it, your hair and eyes are the same color as Lady Eris's, aren't they?"

Kids could be surprisingly perceptive.

Chris was looking a little panicked, but meanwhile, the older girl was also looking studiously at her hair.

...But it wasn't like they'd really caught on to her true identity, right? It was just one of those silly things kids said.

Whatever the girl may have thought, she suddenly held out the flower she was holding. "We have my little sister's flower to offer still, so I want to give this to you. Thank you, adventurer, for always keeping us safe from monsters!"

"Thank you!" her sister added, both of them smiling widely.

"Ah-ha-ha, w-well, this is unexpected. Th-thank *you*; thank you both...!"

Receiving this surprise present from the little girls had made Chris beet red; she struggled to return their smiles as tears welled up at the edges of her eyes.

The girls smiled even wider and ran off. "See you later, Mr. Adventurer!"

"Bye-bye!"

"Huh?! Hey, hold on! I'm not a 'mister.' I'm a 'miss'!"

This second, less pleasant surprise brought fresh tears to Chris's eyes, although for a different reason.

"So tell me. The name Chris…"

Chris brought the flower to her nose, closing her eyes and enjoying the scent.

"That's right. I got it from this flower."

Then, looking happy, she watched the two girls go.

"You're sure you didn't just change one sound from *Eris* to *Chris*."

"Why are you looking at me like that?" Chris glared at me, the flower still pressed to her nose.

"I'm looking at you like…like someone who does everything she can on her own without anybody knowing. The one person I can really respect."

"…Er, oh. Well, uh, I guess that's okay, then." Chris looked away from me quickly, then picked up her pace as if ready to hurry on home.

"Ohhh, are you embarrassed? You're embarrassed, aren't you, Chief?"

"Who's embarrassed? Hush up, Lowly Assistant, and give me a moment to hear myself think."

"When you turn your head away like that, I can see that your ears are bright red. You really are adorable, Lady Eris—will you marry me?"

"You are very loud and very annoying, *Mr.* Kazuma. If you keep teasing the goddess, you're going to bring down divine punishment on yourself. And please don't say such things so nonchalantly—I'll tell Megumin and Darkness that you proposed to me."

Chris still wouldn't look at me, and she was still red up to her ears.

"Say, Lowly Assistant."

"Yeah?"

Chris was walking along with her flower, holding it as if it were a precious treasure.

"...Thanks. For a lot of things."

She was a goddess whose hard work had just been rewarded by two of her smallest believers, and although she spoke quietly, her words were full of emotion.

I went after my friend—my friend whom I couldn't quite resent, who was worth teasing every now and again.

And I was just a little bit sorry that this troublesome, obnoxious festival was over...

One day, well after the end of the festival, when the town had settled down again…

I was lounging on the sofa in the living room, poking at the yellow fuzz ball in the arms of the weirdly realistic empty shell on our couch, when Aqua said happily:

"Hey, Kazuma, I got a thank-you note from Cecily. 'The Axis Church (Axel Branch) has become something wonderful. In addition, the Eris Church has ensured that we will be able to cohost the festival again next year. All of this is thanks to the generous donation from your Mr. Satou. As such, we hereby and entirely on our own recognize him as an honorary Axis disciple.'"

"Graaahhh!"

"Waaaahhh!"

I grabbed the thank-you letter and tore it to pieces.

"You're the worst!" Aqua said. "My precious follower went to all the trouble of writing that letter; how could you hate it enough to do something like that, you brainless NEET?!"

"How could I *not* hate it?! Why should I have to be one of your followers?! That's cruel and unusual punishment!"

In the end, I gave everything I earned as adviser to Aqua. Somehow, when I'd heard that Aqua used not just her entire reward from the hydra but every penny she had been saving up to pay for the festival, I couldn't help feeling a little guilty. I'd also helped in refurbishing the ugly old church, and I thought that pretty much made up for me being behind this whole thing...

"Heh-heh, you're a *tsundere*, Kazuma. And this is how a *tsundere* shows their affection, isn't it? Cecily told me. She said you have a lot of *tsundere* in you, so if you say you hate something, it's really your way of saying you like it."

"I hate you and that lady."

"...Why is it that I don't hear any hint of *tsundere*-ish cuteness when you say that?" Aqua sat down across from me, then tilted her head. "That's right—Kazuma, I wanted to ask you. I heard Eris showed up at that beauty contest. Do you know where she went after that? I can't believe she would come all the way down here and not even say hello to me. As her senior goddess, I'll have to give her a stern talking-to."

In a way, I was perversely impressed that Aqua could continue to act so high and mighty while causing so much trouble for her junior goddess. I stood up from the sofa and plucked Emperor Zel from the arms of Vanir's shell. I had been thinking of everything as pretty much wrapped up, but there was still the question of what to do with this little guy. The chick apparently had plenty of magical energy if nothing else; I wondered if there was some way we could put him to good use.

"Hey, if you treat Emperor Zel like that now, don't be surprised if it costs you later, okay? When he gets big and attacks you, don't expect me to stop him."

"All the more reason to finish him off now, while he's small."

"...It's okay—Emperor Zel is a magnanimous and kind creature, so you don't have to be so scared of him... Come on, Zel; come over here. That man there is as scary as the old butcher in town, so be careful of him."

What old butcher? Who was she talking about?

The emperor was safely back with Vanir's shell and I was lounging again when Darkness came in, rubbing her temples. Apparently, she had been out dealing with gubernatorial business.

"Phew… Work is over at last… I'm really grateful Lady Eris chose to grace us with her presence, but this sudden influx of people…"

"Glad you made it. I guess it's not easy being governor. Lady Eris's appearance has made this town a real tourist trap, huh? But more bodies means a better economy, so that's good for us."

"I'm happy to see more people come through here, but… Anyway, my father completely recovered during the festival. Today was my last day of that awful job as governor, and I want to go on a quest to relax a little."

Darkness looked like she had been freed from a curse.

"Huh? What are you talking about? I'm not working anymore, for real this time, okay? I don't have any reason to. I'm thinking about using my Cooking skill to open a little restaurant, one staffed entirely by cute young women—just as a hobby—but as for quests or whatever, I'm out. You with me, Aqua?"

"You're right. I think I'd better take a break for a while—I want to focus on raising Emperor Zel. I've used up the money Kazuma gave me on rebuilding the church, and funding next year's festival, and also drinking and stuff, but I think I'll keep living the easy life on Kazuma's dime. I won't be going on any dangerous quests. Yes, I think I'd enjoy lying around the house, being venerated at the festival once a year…"

Ah, good to know Aqua agreed with—

"…Hey, wait a second. Why should I have to fund your laziness? I could see covering your meals, maybe, but earn your own pocket change… And are you saying you already spent *everything* I gave you?"

"Uh-huh. But don't you worry about my pocket change. I've got a second and a third great idea for making money."

…

Darkness was irate. "After all the trouble you got into during the festival, you both still…? And you, Aqua, just what kind of ideas do you have? Be absolutely sure you consult with me before you do anything."

"Don't wanna."

………Aqua plugged her ears to block out the lecture Darkness was starting in on.

I cradled Emperor Zel in the palm of my hand as I watched them. Megumin, who must have been up on the second floor, came down wearing her usual dress. She smiled happily to see her friends in one of their familiar arguments, then sat down beside me.

"We worked so hard to make that festival happen, only to have it end with us still sort of flailing about and without any especially fun events. I suppose that's very much like us," she said.

"No kidding," I answered. "The festival was supposed to be crazy and fun and even romantic. And here we got some pitiful fireworks display and had to fight off a bunch of monsters. I wish it had gone on a little longer. I would have liked to at least have a proper fireworks show."

I couldn't resist complaining a little, remembering how nicely things had seemed to be going for me around the time of that fireworks display.

Megumin giggled. "…By the way. Kazuma, you said it was your birthday, right? I must give you a present."

"Aww, don't worry about it. But I admit I'm curious what it would be. Not some weird rock like Aqua gave me, right?"

I spoke jokingly, but Megumin leaned in and whispered in my ear.

"Will you come to my room tonight? I have something important to tell you."

Afterword

I'm your light novelist who can touch his elbow to his chin, Natsume Akatsuki.

Thank you so much for purchasing Volume 8!

Sometimes I just like to take a breather, so this volume might seem a bit all over the place. For those of you thrilled that we've finally got some proper harem light-novel developments, all I'll say is remember what series you're reading and don't get too excited.

You never know if our protagonist, having finally reached the pinnacle of his romantic popularity, might suddenly get struck by a meteor and we might shift to an "MC high-velocity harem" novel starting next volume, like *The Hero Mitsurugi of the Enchanted Blade* or *Strongest Demon Legend Vanirmild*.

While it might not be *Strongest Demon Legend*, The Sneaker WEB is currently serializing a spin-off piece, *May There Be Consultation with This Masked Demon!* so I hope you'll check it out and enjoy.

The other day, I went to take a little look at where they record the anime. The studio is full of machines that make you unconsciously want to play with them, and I was a little fidgety the whole time, but I managed to be an adult and not get in the way, I think.

The whole place was amazing, though. Simply amazing.

The people who can make requests so unreasonable that you think they must be toying with the actors are amazing.

And the actors, who can receive those ridiculous requests and still do a perfectly good job, are amazing.

And sometimes you wonder why a famous actor was wasted on a particular role, and that feeling is amazingly intense, too.

In short, there are plenty of cast members besides those who have already been announced, and I hope you'll look forward to finding out who they are!

Also, I'll apparently be doing an autograph session to commemorate the start of the anime. My handwriting sucks, and I'm not very good in social situations, so I was starting to think my options consisted of (1) playing dead or (2) running away to the countryside, but then they used that killer phrase—"It's for the readers who have supported you for so long"—and I've been practicing my signature ever since.

Once again, I have to thank Kurone Mishima-sensei, my editor S, and everyone else who got this volume safely into print.

Above all, you readers have my deepest thanks for picking up this book!

Natsume Akatsuki

CONGRATULATIONS ON THE RELEASE OF VOLUME 8!
Looking forward to the anime!

MASAHITO WATARI

This happens all the time. I'm not expecting much...

Not expecting much of what?

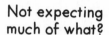

...Maybe I'm expecting just a little, tiny bit.

A little, tiny bit of what?

• • • • • •

I want to tell you something I've been keeping to myself for a very long time.

KONOSUBA: GOD'S BLESSING ON THIS WONDERFUL WORLD! 9

...I mustn't get my hopes up; I mustn't get my hopes up; I mustn't get my hopes up... (mutter)

COMING SOON!!

KONOSUBA SPIN-OFF:

MAY THERE BE CONSULTATION WITH THIS MASKED DEMON!

ALSO COMING SOON!!